pROSE

THOMAS BERNHARD

PROSE

TRANSLATED BY MARTIN CHALMERS

LONDON NEW YORK CALCUTTA

 GOETHE-INSTITUT

This publication was supported by a grant from the Goethe-Institut India

Seagull Books 2010

Prosa
© Suhrkamp Verlag, Germany, 1967

Published for the first time in English by Seagull Books 2010

Translation © Martin Chalmers 2010

ISBN 978 1 9064 9 756 9

British Library Cataloguing-in-Publication Data
A catalogue record for this book is available
from the British Library

Typeset and designed by Seagull Books, Calcutta, India
Printed at Graphic Prints, Calcutta

coNtents

Two Tutors   1

The Cap   15

Is it a Comedy? Is it a Tragedy?   47

Jauregg   65

Attaché at the French Embassy   91

The Crime of an Innsbruck Shopkeeper's Son   103

The Carpenter   131

Afterword: *Crime Stories*   *171*

t<u>w</u>o t*u*Tors

While the new tutor has until now remained
silent during our lunchtime walk, which to me
has already become a habit, today from the start
he had a need to talk to me. Like people who for
a long time have said nothing and suddenly feel it
to be a terrible lack, as something alarming to
themselves and the whole of society linked to
them, he explained to me all at once, agitatedly,
that, really, he always wanted to speak, but could
not speak, talk. I was no doubt familiar with the
circumstance, that there are people, in whose

presence it is impossible to speak . . . In my presence, it was so difficult for him to say anything that he was afraid of every word, he did not know why, he could investigate it, but such an effort would probably vex him over far too long a period of time. Especially now, at the beginning of term, under the pressure of hundreds of pupils, all of them hostile to discipline, under the pressure of the ever coarsening season, he could not afford the least vexation. 'I permit myself absolutely nothing now,' he said, 'I consist one hundred per cent only of my personal difficulties.' Although or precisely because I was a person who, so it appeared to him, had the greatest understanding for him, at my side he was always condemned, at best, as he put it, to make 'ridiculous, indeed embarrassing remarks', yes, or condemned to absolute silence, which caused him continuous torment. For weeks now we have been going for walks side by side and haven't conducted a single conversation. It is true that

we, the new tutor and myself, the old one, have
been able, until this moment, to manage a single
conversation; the remarks on the unusual
weather conditions, on colours, the egoism of nature, abrupt excesses on the surface of the Alpine
foothills, on books, read and unread, intentions,
lack of intentions, on the catastrophic lack of interest of all pupils in their studies, on our own
lack of interest, on eating and sleeping, truth and
lies, chiefly, however, on the most shabby neglect,
on the part of those responsible, of the forest
paths on which we walk, are not conversations;
our remarks destroy our will to converse, our remarks, like remarks altogether, the 'attempts at
capturing the moment', as he calls them, have
nothing to do with the idea of conversation. Here
on the Mönchsberg we make, as we walk, *walking and thinking*, each for himself and completely
isolated, hundreds of remarks, but we have not
yet succeeded in having a conversation, we do
not tolerate a conversation. Because we are who

we are, there is no lack of topics of conversation, but we do not permit ourselves to deploy them for purposes of pure entertainment. Since the beginning of term we walk with each other, beside each other, as if above the dreadful school accumulations, and have not conducted a single conversation. We prevent conversation as if we loathe it. Conversation as the expression of the most absurd human miseries is not possible for us. As far as conversation is concerned we are both such characters who must avoid it in order to save ourselves in a totalitarian madness from being frightened to death. Today, too, no conversation came about. We walk well outside the town and above it and in the middle of it through a grotesque alpine limestone flora, constantly at the mercy of critical observation and constantly making critical observations. The soothing effect of a conversation—we do not permit ourselves such a thing. In fact what the new tutor during our walk today had initially taken the liberty of judging a 'confession', he already described, after only a couple of sentences, as if he wanted from the outset to prevent any intervention on my part in this 'confession', to make it impossible, as merely a remark. Today's remark, however, is of the greatest importance. With respect to his person, and with respect above all to the relationship between him and myself, today's remark by the new tutor proves to be the most revealing.

The new tutor joined me under the windows of the great dormitory after morning lessons. He was pale from overexertion, but did not complain. His undemanding nature occupied my thoughts in the most painful way as we rapidly made progress, finally coming almost to the walls of the brewery, where he suddenly began to talk of his earliest childhood and then immediately of the sleeplessness, which is very closely related to his earliest childhood. This inconsiderately inborn sleeplessness was worsening indeed with

time and there was no remedy for it. It was absurd
to suddenly say now, that he suffered from sleeplessness, *everything* was absurd, and that his sleeplessness was that absolute brain- and body-
destroying sleeplessness, *the* cause of death for
him, for his confession, however, 'for what fol-
lows', it was, he could no longer remain silent
about it, indispensable.

   'If you can imagine,' he said, 'that already as
a child I had to lie in bed awake for ten, twelve
nights in a row, dead tired, without being able to
sleep. An adult,' he said, 'can, thanks to his intelligence, control his sleeplessness, make it ridiculous. Not a child. A child is at the mercy of
sleeplessness.' Above the New Gate, without as
usual looking down vertically on the town, we
turned, as every day, to the right, not to the left:
he wants to turn right, turns right, so I also turn
right, because at this point above the New Gate
he has always turned right, he now no longer
dares turn left, I think . . . It is up to me, one day
to turn left, then he too will turn left, follow me,

8

because he is the weaker of the two of us. . . For
the same reason I have now for weeks been following him to the right . . . Why? The next time
I'll simply turn left, then he too will turn left . . .
The time when I can be useful to him when as
usual I allow him to turn right, follow him to the
right, is over, I think, now I only harm him, when
I let him turn right and follow him . . . He no
longer has the strength all at once to turn left . . .
Shortly after the fork he said: 'What I said to you
regarding my sleeplessness is related to my discharge from the Innsbruck establishment, in
which, as you know, I was employed until the beginning of the holidays.' He said, 'All my life I
have led only an awful life, and it is my right to
lead an awful life, and this awful life is my sleeplessness . . . But now, the story which led to my
discharge from the Innsbruck establishment. Like
all my stories it begins with my inability to sleep.
I was unable to *fall* asleep. I take many drugs,
but no drug helps me any more. I had,' he said,
'walked for hours along the north bank with my

students. We were all tired. My eyes open, incapable of distracting myself by reading, at the mercy of my lifelong sleeplessness, I was gripped by the most despicable thoughts and said to myself again and again: *they* sleep, *I* don't sleep, *they* sleep, *I* don't sleep, *I* don't sleep, *they* sleep, *I* don't sleep . . . This boarding school silence, this dreadful silence emanating from the dormitories . . . When everyone is asleep, only *I* am not sleeping, *I* am not . . . This tremendous capital in the young people's dormitories, I thought . . . The Föhn conditions which stuff sleep into people and suck sleep out of people . . . The pupils sleep, *I* don't sleep . . . These endless nights when heart and spirit die . . . Profoundly aware that there is no remedy for my sleeplessness, I was unable to fall asleep . . . Just imagine, I haven't been able to sleep for weeks . . . There are people who maintain they don't sleep, but they do. There are some who maintain they haven't slept for weeks, and have always slept excellently . . . But I *really* haven't slept for weeks! For weeks, for months! As my scribblings, my notes, show, I haven't slept for months. I have a thick notebook in which I keep a record of my sleeplessness. Every hour of the night in which I don't sleep is marked by a black stroke, every hour of the night in which I do is marked by a black dot. This notebook,' said the new tutor, 'contains thousands of black strokes and only five or six dots. You will not doubt, I assume, now that you know me, the accuracy with which I keep a record of my sleeplessness. And that night, on account of which I am now once again incensed to such a degree that I fear it could give offence, indeed give you offence, that night after a day full of annoyances, as far as my pupils are concerned, incessant, juvenile nonsense, insufferableness, the unyieldingly perverse rock face of Hafelekar in front of me, I was unable to sleep, unable to fall asleep, not even by enlisting quite the most embarrassing pretexts in my already catastrophic choice of

reading . . . I leafed,' he said, 'quite randomly
through *Fear and Trembling* and through *Ei-
ther/Or* and through the Pascalian thought parti-
cles, as if these were popular masochistic
pharmacology books for cases of quite minor imbecility . . . Then suddenly, at about two in the
morning, at the moment at which my tiredness
could overcome my sleeplessness, I suddenly felt
it: the tiredness began to get the better of the
sleeplessness, I fell asleep, really, I fell asleep, although for a long time, as you know, I had no
longer thought of being able to sleep, had no
longer dared think . . . But hardly had I fallen
asleep, than I woke up again—and was woken by
an animal, by an animal that had come out of the
forest . . . This course of events had already repeated itself for weeks by then . . . I wake up and
I hear the animal, for weeks I hear the animal
under my window . . . in the snow . . . every
night at the same time I hear under my window
the animal in the snow . . . I don't know what

kind of an animal it is, I don't have the strength
to get up and go to the window and look out and
down . . . Even now I don't know what kind of
an animal it was . . . The course of events, that I
was unable to fall asleep, but then fell asleep nevertheless and after that was immediately woken
up by the animal, was repeated, as is shown by
my sleeplessness notes, for exactly thirty-six
nights. On the thirty-seventh night, the same
course of events: I was unable to sleep, unable to
fall asleep, and, while I am still humiliated in the
most terrible way by the thought of being unable
to sleep, of not having fallen asleep, I must, as in
the previous thirty-six nights have fallen asleep
nevertheless, because I suddenly woke up,
awoken by the animal which has stepped onto
the snow beneath my window which, as you
know, is always open, even in the most severe
winter . . . Looking for food . . . Then,' said the
new tutor, 'I got up and released the safety catch
on the revolver which, throughout my career as a

tutor I always have under my pillow, and shot the animal in the head.'

We were now both looking down on the square in front of the brewery. 'Naturally, everyone woke up,' said the new tutor, 'the pupils first, then the tutors, the professors, the headmaster. I observed, I listened, as they pulled the shot animal away from the draw-well, along the wall. The tutors dragged it into the building. I heard my name called. A good shot. Naturally, I instantly handed in my resignation. A good shot. I detest Innsbruck. Here, in Salzburg, I already observe now, however, after only the shortest time, the signs of a new calamity. I expressly ask you, dear colleague,' said the new tutor, 'for forgiveness.'

t<u>He</u> cAp

While my brother, for whom a tremendous career is predicted, is giving lectures in the United States at the most important universities about discoveries in the field of mutation research, on which the scholarly publications in Europe, too, report with an almost alarming enthusiasm, I, weary of the countless institutions in Central Europe specializing in sick human heads, have been allowed to stay in his house and I greatly appreciate that he has without reservation placed the whole building at my disposal. This house, which I had never seen before, inherited from his wife, who died quite suddenly six months ago, has, in the first weeks in which I have been allowed to inhabit it, become, given my innate preference for such old houses, whose proportions, that is, their weights and measures, completely coincide with the general and particular natural harmony, and contrary to all forebodings which for years had been capable of utterly tormenting me and fatally disturbing me even down to the very cells, has become the only possible refuge for my dubious existence.

The first two weeks in the house situated right by the shore of Attersee Lake were such a novelty for me that I breathed freely again; my body began to *live* again, my brain tried itself at acrobatics, with which I had lost touch, and which for a healthy person were no doubt ridiculous, but to me, the sick person, however, nevertheless tremendously encouraging.

Already in my first days in Unterach, as the place in which my brother's house stands is called, I could at least start making connections, all at once again imagine the world as a habit, make some of the terms compliant, the very personal ones, to get my revived thought processes going. Admittedly, in Unterach, too, it was impossible for me to study. Wretchedly, I drew back from my initial attempts, from Chabulas, from Diepold, Heisenberg, from Hilf, Liebig, Kriszat, Sir Isaac Newton, who are, so I believe, indispensable to making any progress in my field of the science of woodland and forestry. Yielding to my sick head, in Unterach, too, I soon limited myself just to tracing pictures, to mere analysis, to the detachment of smaller substances from the greater ones of the history of colour, of the whole current history; once again, as so often, I was rebuked and thrown back from one moment to the next to elementary visual colour instruction. Indeed, I lapsed into the most miserable categories of self-observation and of the colour hysteria, as I call it, *in* me, constantly observing all my ways out, without finding a way out; in Unterach I experienced a continuation, but in a dreadful manner, of my fundamentally no more than animal existence, caused by my head, the overexertion by the material altogether. Because I feared my immediate environment in the house could find out about my condition, I sent all the servants away and ordered them not to enter the house again, until my brother was back from America and everything was as usual again. I tried to arouse no suspicion whatsoever with respect to my illness, to my *pathological nature*. The people complied and went away satisfied, overpaid and cheerful. When they were gone and I no longer had any cause to control myself, and in this house, among these people, as I must admit, I had been forced to control myself uninterruptedly in the most dreadful way, as I now calculate, control myself for two weeks, I instantly gave way to my conditions. I closed all the shutters at the front of the house, so that I

didn't have to look out any more. It would have
been absurd to close the shutters at the back, because the windows there looked out onto the
high forest. With open shutters and windows a
far greater darkness entered the house from the
high forest than if they were closed. I left open
only the shutters and windows of the room in
which I spent my time. My room has always had
to have an open window, if I did not want to feel
that I was suffocating. In fact, once I was alone
in the house I immediately made a second attempt to continue my studies, but already in the
first moments of my study of the theory of Dr
Mantel, which I had unwarrantably neglected, I
had known that my efforts would end in a fiasco.
Degraded to the existential minimum of my
brain, I was forced to retreat from my own
books and those of my teachers. The result of
this degradation, which always leads to catastrophic conditions at the back of my head, is
that I can bear nothing any more. Always close

to going completely mad, but not *completely* mad, I then control my brain only to the extent of horrible commands of my hands and feet, for special ordinations on my body. But what I most feared in this house and of which I did not report the least thing to my brother in America, on the contrary, I wrote to him twice a week, as agreed, I was doing well, I was grateful to him, I was making progress with my studies as with my health, I *loved* his house and everything around it, but what I most feared in Unterach, was the twilight, and the darkness which quickly followed after twilight. It's about this twilight that I'm talking here. About this darkness. *Not about the causes* of this twilight, of this darkness, not about its *causalities*, but solely about how this twilight and this darkness in Unterach affect me. But as I see it, at the moment I don't at all have the strength to concern myself with this subject as a problem, as a problem for me, and I want to restrict myself only to outlines, and altogether I want to limit myself solely to the twilight in Un-

terach and to the darkness in Unterach in rela-
tion to me in the condition in which I find myself
in Unterach. I have, after all, no time whatsoever
for a study, because my head, because the sickness of my head, claims the whole of my attention, the whole of my existence. In my room I
cannot bear the twilight and the darkness following the twilight in Unterach, consequently, every
day, when the twilight draws in the darkness in
this ghastly mountain atmosphere, I run out of
my room and out of the house onto the road. I
then have only three possibilities: either to walk
in the direction of Parschallen or in the direction
of Burgau or in the direction of Mondsee. But I
have never yet walked in the direction of Mondsee, because I fear this direction, the whole time
I've only walked in the direction of Burgau; but
today, all at once, I walked in the direction of
Parschallen. In the twilight (here already very
early, already at half past four!), because of my
illness, my cephalalgy, which has been tormenting me now for four years, I was out of my room

into the hall into the darkness onto the road, and because, obeying a sudden signal from my head, I wanted to inflict even greater torture on myself than on preceding days, not towards Burgau, as has been my habit since staying in Unterach, but towards the ugly village of Parschallen, where there are eight butchers, although there are less than a hundred people in the village, just imagine: eight butchers and less than a hundred people . . . I wanted to induce not only the Burgau exhaustion but the much greater Parschallen exhaustion, I wanted to sleep, to *fall* asleep, to at last fall asleep once more. But now, because I have resolved to write down these sentences, there can be no further thought whatsoever of falling asleep. For today a Parschallen exhaustion appeared to me advantageous, so I walked in the direction of Parschallen. In Unterach, my illness has again come to a climax, it now makes me mad in such a way that I am afraid, with total disregard for my beloved travelling-around-in-

America brother, I could hang myself from a tree, go into the water; the ice is still thin, and one goes under right away. I can't swim, that's also to my advantage . . . I have for weeks, it's the truth, been considering killing myself. But I lack resolve. But even if I finally decided to hang myself or to drown myself in a stretch of water, I would be very far from hung, I would also be very far from drowned. A tremendous feebleness and consequently uselessness holds sway over me. Yet the trees practically offer themselves to me, the water pays me court, it tries to draw me in . . . But I walk, I run back and forward, and I don't jump into any water, I don't hang myself from any tree. Because I don't do what the water wants, I am afraid of the water, because I don't do what the trees want, I am afraid of the trees . . . I am afraid of everything . . . And on top of that, it has to be imagined, I go out walking in my only jacket, which is a summer jacket, without a coat, without a waistcoat, in my summer

trousers and in summer shoes . . . But I don't
freeze to death, on the contrary, everything in me
is constantly agitated by a terrible heat, I am pro-
pelled by the heat in my head. Even if I were to
walk to Parschallen completely naked, I could
not freeze to death. To come to the point: I
walked to Parschallen because I don't want to go
mad; I must get out of the house if I don't want
to go mad. But the truth is that I *want* to go
mad, *I want to go mad*, nothing I want more
than to *really* go mad, but I fear that I am far
from being *able* to go mad. I at last want to go
mad! I don't want to be only afraid of going
mad, I at last want to go mad. Two doctors, one
of whom is a highly scientific doctor, have prophesied that I shall go mad, very soon I would go
mad, the two doctors prophesied, very soon, very
soon; now I've been waiting two years for it to
happen, to go mad, but I still haven't gone mad.
But I think, in the twilight and in the sudden
darkness, all the time, that I, if in the evening in

my room, if in the whole house I no longer see anything, if I no longer see what I touch, admittedly *hear* a great deal, but don't *see*, hear and hear *how*, but see nothing, if I would bear this dreadful state of affairs, would bear the twilight and the darkness in my room or at least in the hall or at least somewhere in the house, if I, regardless of the indeed unimaginable pain, would on no account leave the house, that I then *must* go mad. But I shall never bear the state of twilight and the sudden darkness, I will again and again have to run out of the house, as long as I am in Unterach, and I shall be in Unterach until my brother is back from America, is back from Stanford and Princeton, is back from all the North American universities, until the shutters are opened again, the servants are in the house again. I will *have* to run out of the house again and again . . . And it happens like this: I can no longer bear it and run out, I lock all the doors behind me, all my pockets are then full of keys, I

have so many keys in my pockets, especially in
my trouser pockets, that when I walk I make a
frightful noise, and not only a frightful noise, a
dreadful jangling, the keys pound, when and as I
walk, when I chase over to Burgau or, as this
evening, to Parschallen, my thighs and my stomach, and those in my jacket pockets pound my
hips and injure my pleura, because, due to the
great speed which I must attain immediately after
leaving the house, they *obstruct* my restless body,
from the trouser pocket keys alone I have several
injuries, now even suppurating wounds on my
stomach, above all, because in the darkness I
again and again slip, fall on the brutally frozen
ground. Although I have now walked up and
down these roads hundreds of times, I still fall
down. The day before yesterday I fell four times,
last Sunday twelve times, and, something I only
noticed at home, injured my chin; with my
headache I didn't even notice my chin ache at all,
so one can imagine how severe my headache is, if

it was able to suppress this chin ache, caused by a deep wound on my lower jaw. In the large mirror in my room, in which, when I come home, I immediately ascertain the degree of my exhaustion, my *bodily exhaustion*, my *mental exhaustion*, my *daily exhaustion*, I then saw the chin injury (I should of course have had such an injury sewn up by a doctor, but I didn't go to see a doctor, I shall never go to a doctor again, I detest doctors, I shall leave this chin wound as it is), at first not even the chin wound itself, but a large quantity of dried blood on my jacket. I was alarmed when I saw the bloody jacket, because now, it went through my head, the only jacket I have is bloody. But, I immediately said to myself, I go out onto the road only at twilight, only in darkness, so not a soul sees that my jacket is bloody. But I *know* that my jacket is bloody. I didn't even try to clean my bloody jacket. Still in front of the mirror I burst out laughing, and during this laughter I saw that I had cut my chin,

that I was walking around with a serious physical injury. Odd, the way you look with a cut
chin, I thought to myself, when I saw myself in
the mirror with the cut chin. Aside from the fact
that this chin wound disfigured me, my whole
person had all at once an obvious touch of the
ridiculous as well, of the absolute human comedy, and on the way home I had, without knowing it, wiped with my hands blood from the chin
wound all over my face right up to my forehead,
into my hair! I had also torn my trousers. But as
has been said, that was last Sunday, not today,
and I want to say that today on the way to
Parschallen I found a cap and that I am now, as
I'm writing this down, wearing this cap, yes, I am
for various reasons wearing the cap . . . this grey,
thick, coarse, dirty cap, I have already been wearing it for so long, that it has already taken on the
smell of my body . . . I put it on, because I didn't
want to look at it any more. Once I was back
home, I wanted to hide it in my room, hide it in

the hall, for reasons which will probably, even in future, remain completely unclear. I wanted to hide it anywhere at all in the house but I was unable to find a suitable place for it, so I put it on. I didn't want to look at it any longer, but was also unable to throw it away, to destroy it. And now I have been walking around the house for several hours with the cap on my head, without having to look at it. I have spent all of the last few hours under the cap, because I was already wearing it on the way home and only removed it for a moment to find a suitable place for it, and since I didn't find a suitable place for it, I simply put it on again. But I will also be unable always to have the cap on my head . . . In truth, I have already been under the sway of this cap for a long time now, all the time I have thought of nothing else but the cap on my head . . . I fear that this state of affairs, of having the cap on my head and of being under the sway of the cap on my head, down to the smallest and very smallest possibilities of existence of my mind as of my body, mark you, *as* of my body, and being unable to take it from my head, to keep it on and *not* take it off, is connected to my illness, I suspect that: to this illness which so far altogether nine doctors have been unable to explain to me, nine doctors, mark you, whom I had all consulted in the final months before, two years ago, I put a stop to the doctors. Often I could only reach these doctors under the most unimaginably difficult conditions, involving the most tremendous costs. On this occasion I became acquainted with the impertinence of doctors. But, I now think, I have been wearing the cap all evening and I don't know *why* I've been wearing it! And I haven't taken it from my head and don't know *why*! It is a terrible burden to me, as if a smith had forged it to my head. But that is all of minor importance, because I merely wanted to note how I came by the cap, where I found the cap, and, of course, why it is still on my head . . . All of that could be said

in a single sentence, as everything can be said in a
single sentence, but no one is able to say everything in a single sentence . . . Yesterday, at this
time, I had not yet known anything at all about
the cap and now the cap holds sway over me . . .
Furthermore, it's a quite ordinary cap, one of
hundreds of thousands of caps! But everything
that I think, that I feel, that I do, that I *don't* do,
everything that I am, that I represent, is under
the sway of this cap, everything that I am is
under the cap, all at once (for me, *for me in Unterach*!) everything depends on this cap, on one
of these caps, as they are worn, I know, in particular by the butchers of the district, on this
coarse, thick, grey cap. It doesn't absolutely have
to be a butcher's cap, it can also be a woodcutter's cap, the woodcutters also wear these caps,
the farmers too. Everyone here wears these caps.
But finally to get to the point: it began with me
not starting out on the shorter walk to Burgau
but on the longer one to Parschallen, why yester-

day of all days I went not towards Burgau but towards Parschallen, I do not know. All at once instead of turning right, I turned left and towards Parschallen. I have a great dislike of Parschallen. Burgau is ugly, not Parschallen. Likewise the people in Burgau are ugly, not in Parschallen. There's a terrible stench in Burgau, not in Parschallen. But for my conditions Burgau is better. Despite that today I walked to Parschallen. And then on the way to Parschallen I found the cap. I stepped on something soft, at first I thought on a carcass, on a dead rat, on a crushed cat. Whenever I step on something soft in the darkness, I think I have stepped on a dead rat or a crushed cat . . . But perhaps it is not a dead rat at all, I think, not a crushed cat at all, and I take a step backwards. With my foot I push the soft thing into the middle of the road. I establish that it is neither a dead rat nor a crushed cat, not a carcass at all. What is it then? If it's not a carcass, what is it then? No one observes me in the darkness. A movement of the hand and I know it's a cap. A cap with a brim. A cap with a brim such as the butchers, but also the woodcutters and the farmers of the district have on their heads. A cap with a brim, I think, and now all of a sudden I have such a cap with a brim, such as I have always observed on the heads of the butchers and the woodcutters and the farmers, in my hand. What to do with the cap? I tried it on and it fitted. Agreeable, such a cap, I thought, but you cannot put it on because you are neither a butcher nor a woodcutter nor a farmer. How sensible those who have such caps on are, I think. In this cold! Perhaps, I think, one of the woodcutters, who make so much noise cutting wood at night that I can hear it even in Unterach, has lost it? Or a farmer? Or a butcher? Probably a woodcutter. *Definitely* a butcher! This guessing about who could have lost the cap agitated me. To make matters worse I was also occupied by the thought: what is the colour of the cap? Is it black? Is it green? Grey? There are green and black and gray . . . if it's *black* . . . if it's *grey* . . .

green . . . in this terrible guessing game I find myself still on the same spot at which I found the
cap. How long has the cap already been lying on
the road? How agreeable this cap is on my head,
I thought. Then I kept it in my hand . . . If someone sees me with the cap on my head, I thought,
in the darkness which prevails here because of
the mountains, because of the mountains and the
water of the lake, he will take me to be a butcher
or a woodcutter or a farmer. People are immediately taken in by clothing, by caps, jackets, coats,
shoes, they don't see a face, not the walk, no motion of the head, they notice nothing but the
clothing, they see only the jacket and the trousers
into which one has slipped, the shoes and above
all, of course, the cap one is wearing. So for who-
ever sees me with this cap on my head I am a
butcher or a woodcutter or a farmer. So I, who
am neither a butcher nor a woodcutter nor a
farmer, am not permitted to keep the cap on my
head. That would be deceit! An imposture!

Breaking the law! Suddenly, everyone would believe I was a butcher, not a forestry researcher, a
farmer, not a forestry researcher, a woodcutter,
not a forestry researcher! But how can I still describe myself as a forestry researcher when for
more than three years I have no longer been car-
rying out forestry research, I have left Vienna, I
have left my laboratory, I have quite abandoned
all my scholarly, my forestry contacts, by leaving
Vienna I have also left, had to abandon forestry
research, and did so as an unfortunate victim of
my own head. It is three years since I rushed
away from my astonishing experiments into the
hands of the head specialists. That I've rushed
from one head clinic to the next. Altogether in
the last, I can say, four years I have only spent
my life in the hands of every possible kind of
head specialist, spent it in the most pitiful way.
And, indeed, I consist today only of the pieces of
advice of all my head specialists, even if, admittedly, I no longer consult them. I exist thanks to

the thousands and hundreds of thousands of medicines which my head specialists have prescribed for me, on these hundreds and thousands of medicine suggestions! I inject my possibility of existence day in day out at the times specified by just these head specialists! I have my injection apparatus in my pocket all the time. No, I am no forestry researcher any more, I am no research personality any more, I am no research *character* at all any more . . . At twenty-five years of age I am nothing more than a sick man, *nothing more at all*! Nevertheless, precisely because of that I do not have the right to put this cap on my head. I have no right to this cap! And I thought: What is to be done with this cap? I was thinking it all the time. If I keep it, it's theft, if I leave it lying, it's contemptible, so I may not put it on and wear it on my head! I must find the man who lost it, I said to myself, I shall go to Parschallen and ask every man, whether he has lost this cap. First of all, I said to myself, I shall call on the butchers.

Then on the woodcutters. Finally, on the farmers.
I imagine how frightful it is to have to consult all
the men of Parschallen, and walk into
Parschallen. There are many lights, because in
the slaughter rooms the activity has now reached
a climax, in the slaughter rooms and in the
slaughterhouses and in the stalls. Holding the cap
in my hand I walk into the place and knock at
the first butcher's door. The people are—no one
opens—in the slaughter room, I can hear that. I
knock a second time, a third time, a fourth time.
I hear nothing. Finally I hear steps, a man opens
the door and asks what I want. I say, I had found
the cap I'm holding, had he lost the cap, I ask.
'This cap,' I say, 'I found it just outside the village. This cap,' I repeat. Now I see that the cap is
grey, and at this moment I see, that the man
whom I'm asking, whether he has lost the cap
I'm holding in my hand, has exactly the same hat
on his head. 'So,' I say, 'of course you haven't
lost your cap, because you have it on your head.'

And I apologize. The man no doubt took me for
a rascal, because he slammed the door in my
face. With my chin wound I must also have
seemed suspicious to him, the proximity of the
prison did the rest. But surely one of the butchers
has lost it, I think and knock at the next
butcher's. Again a man opens up to me, he also
has such a cap on his head, also a grey one. He
has, he says immediately, when I say, whether he
has perhaps lost his cap, as I can see, his cap on
his head, 'a superfluous question' therefore, he
said. It seemed to me that the man thought my
question, whether he had lost his cap, a trick on
my part. The criminals in the countryside have
the front door opened on some pretext and it's
enough, as one knows, to glance into the hall in
order to get some orientation for later burglaries,
etc. My half-urban, half rural accent aroused the
very greatest suspicion. The man, who seemed to
me far too thin for his trade (a mistake, because
the best, that is, the most ruthless butchers are

thin), pushed me, with the palm of his hand,
which he placed on my chest, back into the darkness. He detested people who are young, strong,
in addition intelligent but work-shy, said the
man, and he confirmed his contempt in the most
wordless butcher's way by raising his hat and
spitting on the ground in front of his boots. At
the third butcher's my call took the same course
as with the first, at the fourth almost exactly the
same course as with the second. Do I have to say
that every one of the Parschallen butchers had
the same grey, coarse, thick cap, cap with a brim
on his head; not one had lost his cap. But I did
not want to give up and rid myself in the most
mean way of the cap I had found (simply by
throwing away the cap), and so I set about call-
ing on the woodcutters. But none of the woodcutters had lost his cap—all of them were
wearing, as they appeared in the doorway to
open up for me (in the darkness in the country,
the men are pushed to the front door by their

wives), a cap with a brim such as I had found. Finally, I also called on all the Parschallen farmers but none of the farmers had lost his cap either. The last to open up for me is an old man, who has the same cap on and asks me what I want, and, when I tell him, he literally forces me, more by his silence than by his dreadful words, to go to Burgau and ask the Burgau butchers whether one of them had lost this cap. An hour ago, he said, seven butchers from Burgau had been in Parschallen and had bought up all the piglets ready for slaughtering. The Burgau butchers paid better prices in Parschallen than the Parschallen butchers, on the other hand, in Burgau the Parschallen butchers paid better piglet prices than the Burgau butchers and so the Parschallen pig farmers have always sold their piglets to the Burgau butchers, on the other hand, the Burgau pig farmers have always sold their piglets to the Parschallen butchers. On leaving Parschallen one of the Burgau butchers had no doubt lost his cap in the piglet tumult, said the old man and slammed the door. This dirty old face with its black spots occupied me all the way to Burgau. Again and again I saw the dirty face and the black spots on it, livor mortis I thought: the man is still alive and already has livor mortis in his face. And, I thought, since the man knows that I have the cap, I have to go to Burgau. Whether I want to or not I have to go to Burgau. The old man will give me away. And I heard all the time, as I walked, the words CAP THIEF, again and again the words CAP THIEF, CAP THIEF. Completely exhausted, I arrived in Burgau. The houses of the butchers in Burgau are all close together. When, however, the first master butcher appeared at the door in response to my knocking and had the same cap on his head as the Parschalleners, I took fright. I instantly turned tail and ran to the next. Here, however, events took the same course—except the man didn't have his cap on, but only, like me, in his hand, so

I didn't ask him either whether perhaps he had
lost his cap . . . But what do I say about why I've
knocked? I thought. I asked what the time was,
and after the butcher had said 'eight o'clock' he
called me an idiot and left me standing. Finally, I
had asked all the butchers in Burgau whether
they had lost their cap, but none had lost his. I
resolved to call on the woodcutters as well, although my situation was already the most agonizing one can imagine. But the woodcutters also
all appeared at the door with the same cap on
their head; the last one even threatened me, because I, frightened, as may be imagined, by his
demand that I disappear immediately, had not
immediately disappeared, and he whacked his
cap on my head and pushed me to the ground.
Each one has the same cap on, I said to myself,
as I set off back home to Unterach, 'each with
the same cap, each one,' I said. Suddenly I was
running, and I didn't even feel that I was running, into Unterach, and I heard from all sides:

'You must give back the cap! You must give back
the cap!' Hundreds of times I heard this sentence:
'You must give it back to its owner!' But I was
too exhausted to ask a single person whether he
perhaps had lost the cap I had found. I had no
more strength left. I would still have had to go to
dozens of butchers and woodcutters and farmers.
Also, it occurred to me, as I entered the house,
that I had seen locksmiths and bricklayers with
such a hat. And who knows, whether someone
from a quite different province than Upper Austria has not lost it. I would still have to ask hundreds, thousands, even hundreds of thousands of
men. Never, I think, was I so exhausted as at the
moment when I decided to keep the cap. Everyone has such a cap on, I thought, everyone, as in
the hall I gave myself up entirely to my dangerous weariness. Again I had the feeling that I had
come to the end, come to the end with myself. I
was afraid of the empty house and of the empty
cold rooms. I was afraid of myself, and it was

only in order no longer to frighten myself to
death in this fatal way which was all my own
that I sat down and wrote these few pages . . .
While I once again gave myself up, even if very
skilfully, nevertheless dreadfully to my sickness
and *pathological nature*, I thought, what will I
do now? and sat down and began to write. And
all the time as I wrote, I thought only that when I
was finished, I would cook something for myself,
eat something, I thought, at last eat something
warm again, and because I had grown so cold
while I was writing, I suddenly put the cap on.
Everyone has such a cap on, I thought, everyone,
as I wrote and wrote and wrote . . .

is iT a c<u>o</u>mEdy?

i<u>S</u> it A TraGed<u>y</u>?

Not having been to the theatre any more for weeks, I had wanted to go to the theatre yesterday, but already two hours before the start of the performance, in my room, therefore, even as I was still engaged in my scholarly work, it was not quite clear to me whether in the foreground or the background of the medical sphere, and which I must at last bring to a conclusion, less for the sake of my parents than my overstrained head, I wondered whether I should not after all do without going to the theatre.

I haven't been to the theatre any more for eight or ten weeks, I said to myself, and I know why I haven't been to the theatre any more, I despise the theatre, I hate the actors, the theatre is nothing but a perfidious impertinence, an impertinent perfidiousness, and suddenly I'm supposed to go to the theatre again? To a play? What does that mean?

You know that the theatre is a nasty business, I said to myself, and you are going to write your study on the theatre, which you've got in your head, this theatre study, which will hit theatre where it hurts once and for all! What the theatre *is*, what the actors *are*, the playwrights, the theatre managers and so on . . .

I was more and more dominated by the theatre, less and less by pathology, a failure in my attempt to ignore the theatre, to forge on with pathology

A failure! A failure!

I dressed and went out into the street.

It is only a half-hour walk to the theatre. During this half hour it became clear to me that it was *impossible* for me to go to the theatre, that going to a theatre, a theatrical performance, was once and for all out of the question for me.

When you've written your theatre study, I thought, then it will be time, then it will be permissible for you to go to the theatre again, so that you can see, that your treatise is *right*!

It was only embarrassing to me that it could have come to this at all, that I bought myself a theatre ticket—I *bought* the theatre ticket, was not *given* it—and that I have tormented myself for two days with the idea of going to the theatre, of watching a theatrical performance, actors, and behind all these actors to scent a miserable and stinking director (Mr T. H.!) and so on . . . but, above all, that I had *changed* for the theatre. You've *changed* for the theatre, I thought.

The theatre study, one day the theatre study! One describes best what one hates, I thought.

With five, possibly seven, sections, under the title THEATRE—THEATRE? my study will soon be finished. (Once it's finished, you'll burn it, because it's pointless to publish it, you'll read it through and burn it. Publication is ridiculous, *wrong aim*!) First section THE ACTORS, second section THE ACTORS IN THE ACTORS, third section THE ACTORS IN THE ACTORS OF THE ACTORS and so on . . . fourth section STAGE EXCESSES and so on . . . last section: SO, WHAT IS THE THEATRE?

With these thoughts I reached the Volksgarten park.

I sit down on a bench by Café Meierei, although at this time of year to sit down on a Volksgarten bench can be *fatal*, and observe, intently, with pleasure, with tremendous concentration, *who* goes into the theatre and *how* they go into the theatre.

It pleases me, *not* to go in.

But you should, I think, go in and, in view of your poverty, sell your ticket, *go in*, I say to myself, and, while I'm thinking that, I take the greatest pleasure in rubbing away my theatre ticket between the thumb and index finger of my right hand, rubbing away the theatre.

First of all, I say to myself, there are more and more people going into the theatre, then less and less. Finally, no one is going into the theatre any more.

The performance has begun, I think, and I stand up and walk a little way in the direction of the central part of town, I'm cold, I haven't eaten anything and, it occurs to me, not spoken to anyone for more than a week, when I am suddenly addressed: a man has addressed me, I hear a man asking me what the time is, and I hear myself exclaim, 'Eight o'clock.'

'It's eight o'clock,' I say, 'the performance has begun.'

Now I turn around and see the man.

The man is tall and thin.

Apart from this man, there is no one in the Volksgarten park, I think.

Immediately I think that I have nothing to lose.

But to say the sentence: '*I have nothing to lose*!' out loud, to say it *loudly*, seems to me absurd, and I don't say the sentence out loud, although I have a great desire to say the sentence out loud.

He had lost his watch, said the man.

'Ever since I lost my watch, I'm forced to address people from time to time.'

He laughed.

'If I hadn't lost my watch, I would not have addressed you,' he said, 'addressed *no one*.'

He found the observation itself extremely interesting, said the man, that he, after I had told him that it was eight o'clock, now knew, that it *was* eight o'clock and that today he had, for eleven hours uninterruptedly—'without interruption,' he said—been walking with a single thought, 'not up and down,' he said, but 'always straight ahead, yet as I now see,' he said, 'always in a circle. Crazy, isn't it?'

I saw that the man was wearing women's shoes, and the man saw that I had seen that he was wearing women's shoes.

'Yes,' he said, 'you may now wonder about that.'

'I had,' I said quickly, to distract the man and myself from his women's shoes, 'wanted to go to the theatre, but right in front of the theatre I turned round and didn't go into the theatre.'

'I have been in this theatre very often,' said the man, he had introduced himself, but I had forgotten his name, I never remember names, 'one day for the last time, as every man one day goes to a theatre for the last time, don't laugh!' said the man, 'one day everything is for the last time, don't laugh!'

'Oh,' he said, 'what's on today? No no,' he said quickly, 'don't tell me what's on today . . .'

He went to the Volksgarten park every day, said the man, 'since the beginning of the season I always go to the Volksgarten park at this time, so that from here, from this corner, from the Café Meierei wall, you see, I can observe the theatregoers. Curious people,' he said.

'Admittedly, one would have to know what's on today,' he said, 'but don't *you* tell me what's on today. For me it's extremely interesting, for once, *not* to know what's on. Is it a comedy? Is it a tragedy?' he asked and immediately said: 'No no, don't say, *what it is*. Don't say it!'

The man is fifty, or he's fifty-five, I think.

He suggests walking in the direction of the Parliament building.

'Let's go as far as the Parliament building,' he says, 'and back again. It's always remarkably quiet, once the performance has begun. *I love this theatre* . . .'

He walked very quickly, and it was almost unbearable for me to watch him as he did so, the thought that the man was wearing women's shoes made me feel sick.

'Here I take the same number of steps every day, that is,' he said, 'in these shoes I walk from Café Meierei to the Parliament building, to the railings, taking exactly three hundred and twenty-eight steps. In the *buckle* shoes, I take three hundred and ten. And to the Swiss Wing— he meant the Swiss Wing of the Hofburg Palace—I take exactly four hundred and fourteen steps in *these* shoes, three hundred and twenty- nine in the *buckle* shoes! Women's shoes, you may think, and you may find that repulsive, I know,' says the man.

'But then I only go into the street when it's dark. That every evening I go into the Volksgarten park at this time, always half an hour before the beginning of the performance is, as you may imagine, the result of a shock. It is already twenty-two years since this shock. And it is very closely linked to the women's shoes. Incident,' he says, 'an incident. It is quite the atmosphere of those days: the curtain has just gone up in the theatre, the actors are beginning to play, the absence of people outside . . . Let us walk now,' says the man, as we reach Café Meierei again, 'to the Swiss Wing.'

A madman? I thought, as we walked to the Swiss Wing, side by side, the man said: 'The world is entirely, through and through, a juridical one, as you may not know. The world is nothing but a monstrous jurisprudence. The world is a prison!'

He said: 'It is exactly forty-eight days since I last encountered a person at this time in the Volksgarten park. I asked *this* man, too, what the time was. This man, too, told me that it was eight o'clock. Curiously I always ask at eight o'clock, what the time is. This man, too, walked with me as far as the Parliament building and as far as the Swiss Wing. Furthermore,' said the man, 'I have, this is the truth, not lost my watch, I don't lose my watch. Here, look, here's my watch,' he said and held his wrist in front of my face, so that I could see his watch.

'A trick!' he said, 'but to continue: this man, whom I encountered forty-eight days ago, was a man of your age. Like you, taciturn, like you, at first *un*decided, then determined to walk with me. A student of the natural sciences,' said the man. 'I also said to *him*, that a shock, an incident that occurred a long time ago, is the reason for me being here in the Volksgarten park every evening. Wearing women's shoes. Same reaction,' said the man, and: 'Furthermore I have never seen a policeman there. For several days the police have been avoiding the Volksgarten park and concentrating on the City Park, and I know why . . .'

'Now it would indeed be interesting,' he said, 'to know whether at the moment at which we are walking towards the Swiss Wing, a comedy or a tragedy is being performed in the theatre . . . This is the first time that I don't know what is being performed. But *you* must not tell me . . . No, don't say what it is! It should not be hard,' he said, 'by studying *you*, by concentrating entirely on *you*, by concerning myself exclusively only *with you*, to discover whether at this moment a comedy or a tragedy is being performed in the theatre. 'Yes,' he said, 'in time the study of your person will inform me about everything that is happening in the theatre, and about everything that is happening outside the theatre, about everything in the world, which at every moment is entirely linked to you. Finally, at some point, the moment really could arrive at which, by studying you as intensively as possible, I know everything about you . . .'

When we had reached the wall of the Swiss Wing, he said: 'Here, on this spot, the young man, whom I encountered forty-eight days ago, took his leave of me. You want to know, *in what manner*? Careful! Ah!' he said, 'So *you* are not taking your leave? You are *not* saying "Good night"? Yes,' he said, 'then let's go back again from the Swiss Wing to where we started. Now where did we start? Ah yes, at Café Meierei. The curious thing about people is that they constantly mix themselves up with other people. So,' he said, 'you wanted to go to this evening's performance. Although you, as you say, hate the theatre. *Hate* the theatre? I *love* it . . .'

Now it struck me that the man had a woman's hat on his head. All that time I hadn't noticed it.

The coat he was wearing was also a woman's coat, a woman's winter coat.

He really is wearing nothing but women's clothes, I thought.

'In summer,' he said, 'I don't go to the Volksgarten park, there are no performances then, of
course, but always, *when* there are performances
in the theatre, I go to the Volksgarten park, then,
when there are performances in the theatre, no
one else apart from me goes to the Volksgarten
park, because then the Volksgarten park is far too
cold. Young men come singly to the Volksgarten
park, whom I, as you know, immediately address
and ask to walk with me, once as far as the Parliament building, once as far as the Swiss Wing . . .
and from the Swiss Wing and from Café Meierei
always back again . . . But until now not one person, and that is striking,' he said, 'has walked
twice with me as far as the Parliament building
and *twice* as far as the Swiss Wing and therefore
four times back to Café Meierei. Now we have
walked *twice* to the Parliament building and *twice*
to the Swiss Wing and back again,' he said, 'that's
enough. If you like,' he said, 'accompany me a
part of the way home. Never ever has even one

man accompanied me a part of the way home from here.'

He was staying in the Twentieth District.

He was *putting up* in the apartment of his parents, who ('suicide, young man, suicide!') had died six weeks earlier.

'We have to cross the Danube Canal,' he said.

I was interested in the man, and I wanted to accompany him for as long as possible.

'At the Danube Canal you have to turn back,' he said. 'You must not accompany me any further than the Danube Canal. Don't ask *why* until we've reached the Danube Canal!'

Beyond the Rossauer Barracks, a hundred yards before the bridge, which leads over to the Twentieth District, the man suddenly said, having come to a halt, looking down into the water of the canal: 'Yes, at this spot.'

He turned to me and repeated: 'At this spot.'

And he said: 'I pushed her in quick as a flash. The clothes I'm wearing are *her clothes*.'

Then he made a sign that meant: *disappear*!

He wanted to be alone.

'Go!' he ordered.

I didn't go immediately.

I let him finish speaking: 'Twenty-two years and eight months ago,' he said.

'And if you think that it's a pleasure in prison, then you are mistaken! The whole world is a jurisprudence. The whole world is a prison. And this evening, let me tell you, in the theatre over there, whether you believe it or not, a comedy is being performed. *Indeed*, a comedy.'

JAUREGG

My arrival in Jauregg, in the evening, at about eight o'clock, three years ago, gave rise, I think, to hopes which have not been fulfilled, on the contrary, my position has only worsened from the moment I set foot on the soil of Jauregg. One reason why I left the city, after all, had no doubt been the tremendous excess of people, among whom, because of the defencelessness of my physical and nervous centres, my lack of useful possibilities, I virtually threatened to suffocate. The thought, as I woke up every morning, of having to carry out my daily work under the weight of one million seven hundred thousand people, almost killed me. So I saw the sudden decision to leave the city and accept the offer of my uncle, the Master of Jauregg, of joining the main office of his quarries, as a positive turn for my further development. Now, however, I see that conditions in the country are even more oppressive than those in the city, and that four hundred people in the Jauregg Quarries are a much greater weight on the head of a person than one million seven hundred thousand in the city. And if I had thought, in contrast to the conditions in the city where, within a space of almost ten years, making new contacts had no longer been possible for me, to find such in the countryside, so I was soon forced to realize that, by entering into the service of the Jauregg Quarries, I had made a mistake. Here, no contacts are to be made with people, because the conditions which prevail here, and the people who live here in the

Jauregg Quarries, render the making of contacts,
such as I desire, impossible. Above all, the mistrust of everything developed here by each person
as the highest art is to blame for the complete
lack of contact between everyone employed in
the Jauregg Quarries. If in the first hours of my
stay in the quarries I had been certain before long
to have found what I was looking for—contact
with people—I soon realized that it would not be
possible for me to find even one reassuring person to talk to for my long evenings, quite apart
from the sleepless nights. Never before had people treated me with such hurtful rejection as did
those in the Jauregg Quarries. That it is possible
to punish someone, who is helpless and seeking
help, for his helplessness, in, as I think, such a
spiteful way, by not only not allowing him to
come close but each time, at even the slightest attempt to come close, to join them, by obscene silence or to offend him by obscene remarks,
shocked me. At first I believed that their inhuman

behaviour   towards me was due to the fact, or
linked to the fact, that I am a nephew of the
Master of Jauregg, but I soon realized that this, I
must admit, dreadful family relationship plays
absolutely no part in this connection. I neither
lost nor profited by it. I discovered that everyone
is the same to everyone, which for moments, I remember exactly, reassured me, but for the rest of
my stay in the quarries, perhaps, as I fear, for the
whole of my remaining life, cast me into the
greatest unhappiness. One has to know that here,
aside from the natural mechanical-physical as-
pect, there is absolutely no difference at all between men and women; children do not in the
least fulfil the natural purposes of men and
women expected of them, here in the Jauregg
Quarries all are equal, even if younger or older,
then nevertheless completely equal . . . Also their
faces, for that matter, do not differ in the least
from each other, their hopeless physiognomy is
the same, the way they walk, they way they talk,

the way they sleep, continuously procure food.
Everyone wears the grey Jauregg working
clothes, the Jauregg working shoes, the Jauregg
work cap. Everyone is treated in completely the
same way by the Jauregg office system. And they
do not, as elsewhere, where people are together,
behave correspondingly differently in each place,
for example at the workplace and in the canteen,
no, they always behave in the same way. The attempts by the works council, but also by my
uncle, to loosen up the monotonous atmosphere
in the Jauregg Quarries, by, for example, from
time to time engaging a group of folk dancers or
a small circus, or a comedian, like the Styrian
who is appearing tonight, are in vain. For here a
general exhaustion prevails and a general will to
nothing. But these thoughts only distract me
from the one and only thought I have, from uninterruptedly thinking about my uncle. However
much I wish to be distracted from this thought,
day and night I think, whatever else I'm thinking,

whatever else I'm doing, about my uncle and
how I should behave to my uncle, who is guilty
of my mother's death. It is principally this guilt
on my uncle's part for my mother's death which
caused me to go to the quarries . . . Nothing else.
That is the truth. And I think: in the three years
that I've been in Jauregg, I have only once seen
my uncle. I was allowed to attend a lunch which
he gave in the canteen for a businessman from
Vienna, because of a large order which was
thanks to the businessman. During the whole
meal he had not once turned to me and had deliberately not drawn me into the conversation
with his visitors—apart from the businessman
from Vienna, there had been two other gentlemen present, factory owners with whom he was
on friendly terms. At the time I asked myself
why had he let them join me for the meal. Again
and again I asked myself about the reason, without, however, finding one. After he had introduced me to the gentlemen with the words 'My

nephew', my uncle did not as much as look at me
again. The meal, it occurs to me, took place exactly three days after I started work in the quarries. I remember that during the whole meal I
had waited to be asked by my uncle how I was,
at least whether I had settled in yet. Where my
(modest) accommodation was located. Whether I
had been treated obligingly on my arrival. I was
ill at the time, and I said to myself at table, 'Now
that you've taken up his offer and signed the
service contract and started work, he's
"dropped" you.' One has to imagine, the meal
lasted one and a half hours, and my uncle didn't
say a single word to me. No doubt, because he
dominated them without them noticing it, the Viennese gentlemen did not have a word to say to
me either, apart from that discourteousness, they
several times knocked against me under the table
with their feet without the least apology. Why
this meal comes to mind just now, I don't know.
Three years have passed, and not once have I

seen my uncle again, although I know that he
carries out an inspection in the quarries every
two or three weeks. I go out of his way; if I hear
that he's coming, I go to where he won't find me.
If he had summoned me just once!—I think.
There are rooms in the office hut, which he
doesn't enter, indeed, which he doesn't even
know about—that's where I withdraw when he
comes . . . Every time he's gone, when I'm back
in the office, I ask whether my uncle has asked
after me, and every time the answer I get is that
he had not. He's satisfied with my work, because
the chief clerk is satisfied with it. But one day I
shall have to face him and say to him . . . I think
I am afraid of meeting him. I could not remain
silent, but the truth must wound him, if it does
not at least wound him, if I don't at least . . . But,
in fact, I have long ago resigned myself to with-
drawing entirely from him, and the likelihood,
that I suddenly find myself face to face with him,
say everything, only not the truth, don't say what

I think of him, so that I don't wound him, so that I don't even irritate him, that I am then too weak, is greater than the likelihood that, when it matters, I am open and therefore strong . . . If I, within the feebleness which I can no longer escape, just once had the strength, to say to my uncle's face, what I think about him, what, with respect to the relationship between him and my mother, who can now no longer defend herself, I think about him! But it is already an impossibility for me to approach my uncle . . . But why, I think, given all these terrible circumstances and premises, did I accept his offer to work in the quarries? Why am I *here* at all? And, I think, at the point in time, when he made me the verbal offer, to go to the quarries ('Go to my quarries, then!'), I can still hear his paternal-cynical tone, did I not say the truth to his face, and *at that time, not now*, now it's too late, called to mind the shocking truth for all time? Had I already been then, at the chance meeting between myself and my uncle at his brother-in-law's house, a victim of my feebleness? If I, I think, had said nothing in front of the two men about my situation, about my then dreadful mental and physical state . . . Or if I had at least rejected his offer, to take up a post at the quarries, immediately and without hesitation . . . But, no longer master of my despair, I allowed my uncle to look deep inside me . . . Whether out of clumsiness, out of sudden mental and physical weakness, a man like me is constantly opening the door wide to enemies, above all to his enemies. Perhaps it was to punish myself, not my uncle, without knowing for what I was punishing myself, giving myself up to a deadly chastisement, that I accepted my uncle's offer, to sell myself for a humanly most undignified low price into the Jauregg Quarries, and so immediately took up a post in the office . . . Possibly it's precisely this decision of mine, to *give myself up* to my uncle, that is the cause of his contempt for me, which he made me feel so

clearly during the meal for the businessmen from
Vienna . . . It was precisely to be able to show his
contempt for me, that he invited me to the lunch
. . . There is, of course, the possibility, that he expected me to reject his offer to go and work in
the quarries . . . So many possibilities . . . But the
reason for inviting me to the lunch with the businessmen from Vienna was no doubt to wound
me for a long time, perhaps he even intended my
complete destruction . . . In me, he always saw
all the crimes he had committed against my
mother . . . But in order to be able to characterize
my uncle's relationship with my mother more
precisely, my thoughts would have to go far back
into the childhood of both. My brain possesses a
whole archive, divided into hundreds of sections,
concerning this relationship . . . Even before his
birth, my uncle had been predestined by nature,
designated, to systematically destroy my mother's
life, to make her life a dreadful death *on and on
and on.* All the dreadfulness, which nature had

placed in him, my uncle developed, with his great intelligence, slowly and with ever greater refinement into the methodical destruction of his sister, my mother . . . The climax of this destruction concept, destruction process rather, was the night my mother spent with my uncle in the forester's lodge and after which she took her life in the terrible way she did. No one knows what occurred in the forester's lodge that night, and yet in years of sleeplessness I have become familiar with and aware of them down to the smallest detail. Over time, my investigations in this respect have led to dreadful results, to such results, however, which instead of now, finally, as my uncle would deserve, making me capable of taking action, make me completely *incapable* of taking action . . . A degree of shock has now presumably intervened, which has made me completely helpless . . . For a long time now I have only existed in consideration, in examination of what occurred then, on 7 July four years ago in the forester's lodge . . . But

at the same time I exist in a state of helplessnesss
which excludes every activity . . . So it is, that I
am completely at the mercy of the entire ridiculous ordinariness which prevails here . . . And
day and night I ask myself, again and again, day
and night, *whether* one day what *should* happen
will happen . . . What am I looking for here, I
ask myself that uninterruptedly, here, in the Jauregg Quarries, if not everything conceivable
which can be used against the uncle who, as far
back as I can think, I have always hated? No,
under his influence I, too, am being destroyed,
just as, under his influence, my mother was destroyed . . . And I think, while I, as every day, as
is my habit, immediately after office hours, walk
up and down in front of the hut, that, so I think,
today, this dark grey day would drive me to despair, if the Styrian comedian was not coming
this evening, whom I have already seen once before, a talented young man . . . Yesterday, and
once again while I was walking up and down in

front of the hut after office hours, I thought, I would despair if I did not join the card game in the canteen . . . and the day before yesterday, walking up and down in front of the hut in the same way, I looked forward to having my hair cut by the barber and so did not despair. So every day, when office hours are over, something intervenes, which stops me from despairing, although I *should* despair, although in truth I *am* in despair. And although I know that, because in fact I always have something after office hours which *distracts* me, not always something that *pleases* me, at least something that distracts me, I am, every time, afraid before office closing hours. Because one day, I think, it could be that I no longer have anything that gives me pleasure or even distracts me. There is simply no pleasure and no distraction any more—it's a law of nature that for every person there is, one day, no pleasure nor any distraction any more, not the least pleasure, not the most insignificant distraction . . .

And I think, I should, in accordance with the circumstances, which prevail here, in reality, if I consider it, be the most desperate man, and possibly I am the most desperate man, but I think, I walk more quickly, ever more quickly up and down, and I say to myself, you must be desperate, you must be in a state of the greatest despair and you have a right, you have a right to this despair, day in day out, to be desperate again and again, and I think, after office hours, when, suddenly left alone, I walk up and down in front of the hut and no longer know what to do with myself, except to walk up and down, rather, in anticipation of an evening's distraction, diversion, bridging of my aloneness, in the face of my sudden powerlessness, my nausea, that my existence is indeed a desperate existence . . . But I also know that it is ridiculous to lead a desperate existence, even to conclude that one is leading a desperate existence is ridiculous, as the use of the word 'despair' is in itself already ridiculous . . .

and how, if one considers it, *all* words that one uses suddenly become ridiculous . . . but I permit myself no digression, ridiculous or not, my existence is a desperate one, just as there are only desperate existences in the Jauregg Quarries, not a single one that is *not* desperate but, like the others, my existence, too, in accordance with the circumstances in the Jauregg Quarries, has become apathetic, undemanding . . . I tell myself, I may be desperate but I must not despair, fundamentally I am always desperate, definitively, but I do not *have* to despair . . . And I constantly arrange a distraction, a diversion for myself for the coming evening: last Friday, I bought myself a book, last Tuesday something good, something tasty to eat . . . I write letters, I study the natural sciences . . . I multiply and divide, I can distract myself with spiritualist, geo-physical exercises . . . I conduct conversations with myself. For hours I look through the windows into the huts and watch, or I abandon myself to my reflections

in bed. I fear this way of filling up my time, however, because it produces the opposite of a distraction, and leads, depending on the causes,
sooner or later to headaches and nausea. For
variety I walk every evening, without being able
to change the habit, without wanting to change
it, after office hours, but presumably deep under
the surface of the early stages of a mental illness,
of a pure creature illness, which, as I have found
out, has more to do with my father, less with my
mother, up and down, walk up and down on the
closed, completely closed *off* area of the Jauregg
Quarries and always between the office hut and
the hut where the workers live . . . To the workers I am, after five o'clock, separated from them,
by my now, even to myself, astonishing distraction skills, nothing but someone who walks up
down between the huts always at the same pace,
whereas I am indeed after office hours no doubt
someone walking up and down between the huts,
at the same time, however, and with much deeper

awareness, *someone walking up and down in his illness*, someone addicted to his illness as to a strict scientific exercise, who seeks relief through answers loudly called back, greetings to loud questions, greetings to passers-by. Existence in the Jauregg Quarries is difficult, if not quite dreadful . . . A society grown coarse and embittered in the isolation of the Jauregg Quarries must inevitably be met with the greatest adroitness, if a man like myself wishes to maintain himself in it for more than even the shortest period of time. Mistakes once made in front of a crowd of people seeking and finding a way to get by in nothing more than prying and malicious joy, endeavouring to mutually destroy each other, can no longer be made good, the least mistake can be the start of a conspiracy, a martyrdom; how often has such a mistake in the Jauregg Quarries—and I know of so many cases!—a rash remark, a not-quite-considered statement, been the cause of a person's death. The imbecility and

the brutality resulting from the imbecility of the
common Jauregg mass turn each phase of a
course of events which is oppressive to all into a
catastrophe for oneself . . . If I wake up, I resist
everything for so long until I fall asleep. Above
all, I fear being drawn into one of their fatal conversations, for many weeks being *addressed* at
all, being discovered at all. But in order to live
one must be together with people . . . Going
away from the Jauregg Quarries, going out,
going back to the city, I've often thought of it,
but I have not gone away, and I have not gone
back to the city . . . My employment in the Jauregg Quarries led in the shortest time to my almost complete isolation . . . I now no longer have
contact with anyone but myself . . . The cause is
the indeed deadly isolation of the Jauregg Quarries, the high mountains rising up on all sides, the
constant mirage of a fauna terrifying all minds
. . . As for myself, then from the moment at
which I realized that the Jauregg Quarries, in

obedience to nature, are hostile to man, I have no longer had the strength to go away . . . And with what intentions, my mind supposedly healthy and alert, did I come here!—Now I see the comedian, and I take a deep breath, as if I were saved! I only need to follow the man from Styria, I think, still outside I take off my jacket, I throw my hat into the cloakroom . . . I still find one last seat in the crowded canteen . . . The comedian says something, everyone laughs. I think all attempts to resume my earlier life, which after all had been neither hopeless nor monotonous, where I had broken it off, in the city, that is, among all possible people and under all possible conditions, that is, with all possible possibilities, have failed. Today I no longer know why I really left the city and went to the Jauregg Quarries. For the sake of my mother? . . . I torment myself with the answer, which I can no longer give myself, I ask myself: was it the sudden insufferableness of city life? No, nothing, but really nothing at all, that one could explain. Three years have passed in this way without my once having asked myself again, why I *really*, yes, *in reality*, accepted the post in the Jauregg Quarries, why I still *am* in the Jauregg Quarries. Everything, I think, suggests that I shall remain in the Jauregg Quarries for the whole of my life . . . in thoughts always occupied with my uncle . . . with my mother. The head clerk once said, I was a good adder-up of numbers. So I'm a good adder-up of numbers . . . From time to time, I think, I tell a joke I've made up, then my colleagues laugh. They know me as a good teller of jokes. I know of no greater torment than telling a joke, but, since I have no other possibility, I won't say to make my colleagues like me, I mean, just to keep my head above water, I from time to time tell a joke I've made up which they describe as a good joke. But I am not a comedian. For days and nights I think up such a joke. I am not a comedian. If I can tell it, I won't go under. If I tell it

particularly well, for a while I rise in the estima-
tion of my colleagues. But I am not a comedian.
If they had to say who I was, they would then no
doubt say I was a good adder-up of numbers and
an almost as good teller of jokes. But I am not a
comedian. I don't know in what other way I
could still distinguish myself. I never go to the
Jauregg gymnasium, in the swimming pool I
manage only the most timid efforts and I make
myself look ridiculous every time. In the canteen
I always play (the comedian has for some time
now only been comical because of his Styrian accent!) the most absolutely subordinate role. In
telling stories I am too slow and I tell them with
pauses that are far too long. Nor do I stand out
because of a pleasant voice. For example, I can't
whistle. In my clothing I favour that inconspicu-
ousness which others find presumptuous, they
feel that everything I wear is not appropriate for
the Jauregg Quarries. I am now not talking about
the workers, I mean the small-minded, the dull

people in the office, who seem to be constantly reproaching me, who do I think I am and why am I like this and not like *that*, and above all, why I am *at all*. But in reality (now they're laughing again!) here everyone reproaches everyone with everything.

attAché at The fREnch eMbAssY

Holiday Diary, Conclusion

21st Sept.

During supper it became apparent how swiftly a
pleasant mood and company, in this case produced by several causes, individually insignificant
but in their interaction nevertheless decisive, can
suddenly become a sombre one. As if not wishing
to surrender to the horror, which we could not
avoid thinking about as we ate, we feared the
consequences of all thought. The evening meal

had begun punctually in a state of greatest disquiet, in which suppositions and apprehensions had led to a silence terrible not least for the wife of the missing man. My uncle had not come back from his forest inspection. We had searched for him, in vain. (The fact of his absence had such a paralysing effect because, as long as anyone could remember, he had never returned unpunctually from his evening forest inspection.)

As we silently ate supper, I studied above all the behaviour of my uncle's wife. But it is not the description of the tension, indeed the despair of the company at table which, as I know today, inevitably made a connection between my uncle and a series of dreadful accidents, crimes, that interests me now, only what my uncle related when, to everyone's complete surprise, he appeared half an hour after the beginning of the meal.

No one had been expecting him any more, when he entered and sat down at his place as if nothing had happened and said that in the forest,

in the bit of mixed woodland, which borders on
the pine forest, he had, without in the least antici-
pating the encounter, met a young man, 'a fine figure of a young man', as he said. The man had
been very well dressed. Because of the time of day,
my uncle had been unable to see the man's face
but was instantly able to classify his voice as that
of someone of above average intelligence. (From
the very first moment my uncle had felt the encounter with the stranger to be a stroke of luck.)

'It was,' said my uncle, 'oddly enough, as if
for years I had been waiting for nothing else but
this meeting.'

My uncle had not for a moment thought of a
crime, not for a moment of a trap.

He invited the young man, who had mentioned his name and yet remained completely
anonymous, to walk with him for a little.

He had to inspect a number of tree trunks
for their readiness for felling, he preferred com-

pany for that, and he had thought, the man is trustworthy and: 'possibly, he thinks the same way as I do, one can draw conclusions about a person from moods, movements' and so forth.

'This forest,' my uncle had said to the young man, 'is good', then again: 'This wood is bad, and I want to explain to you why *that* wood is good, the other bad. In the darkness, you can't, of course, see why *that* is good and the other bad. But why am I telling you that *that* wood is good and the other bad? ('People!'). It's possible that you're not in the least interested. I, however, have to be constantly interested in these peculiarities, peculiarities of the *land*. These thoughts preoccupy me day and night: Is *this* wood good? Is *this* wood bad? Why is *that one* good? Why is *that one* bad? In daylight you would immediately recognize that *this* wood ('Man!') in which we are now, is bad, and you would be able to say with the same confidence of the one we are entering now, that it is *good*. But now you can make out nothing. The darkness makes it impossible to ascertain whether the wood ('Man!') is good, whether the wood ('Man!') is bad. I know, however, that the wood, in which we are now, is bad, that the wood we are entering now is good. I am familiar with the state of all my woods . . . I see my plots of land day and night . . . Uninterruptedly . . . My plots of land are my subject. I can imagine that a philosopher sees all his philosophies day and night, if he is an ideal philosopher. The art of it is that the philosopher always *sees through* all philosophies, while mine is, always, to *see through* all the plots of land. I have to know whether and *how* the tree is rotten. I have to know what *is* in the tree. Whatever it is, I always have to know it. The world is, as you know, a world of possibilities, my plots of land are plots of land of possibilities, as the philosophies are philosophies of possibilities. We are always thinking in terms of possibilities.'

The young stranger showed himself to be not only interested but knowledgeable as far as the science of woods and forestry was concerned. (As it turned out, the stranger was an expert as far as the whole economic and scientific development of forestry was concerned.)

'What I like so much,' said my uncle, 'the young man quoted *nature itself*, not books *about nature*.'

My uncle took more and more pleasure in the encounter. As he related, the subject of their conversation was soon no longer the science of woods and forestry, but finally, which astonished my uncle, since both of them were so-called *practical men at the height of the twentieth century*, the arts. They had talked about literature. About music. (One of the few young people with whom one can talk about everything, without having to fear at every moment trivializing them *and so also oneself* in the most embarrassing way, the stranger had after only a short time, thanks to his predilections such as those for literature and music, above all, his knowledge concerning nature, been certain of my uncle's sympathy.)

'The young man's German was outstanding, but nevertheless spoken by a foreigner,' said my uncle. A Frenchman! he had thought immediately, yes, a Frenchman! and: *how does a Frenchman come to be in my forest at this time of day*? But then he had said to himself: of course, he must be a French relative of the Minister of Agriculture. The young man had, for whatever reason, and young people have *youthful reasons*, gone for a walk before going to bed; an interest in phenomena, in the peculiarities of a physical, chemical, philosophical nature so numerous in Upper Austria in particular, had caused him to leave the house *at dusk*. Admittedly, a man alone in the forest in the darkness is extremely suspect, not only here, but everywhere in the world. But this thought had not concerned my uncle. 'Trust,' he said, 'mutual trust.'

Not for a moment had my uncle thought of a gun.

'It was at dusk, which is already dark,' he said.

'Odd,' he said, and then: 'After I had told the man about fertilizing and seeding felling, about shade-tolerant species and a very interesting story about the Weymouth pine, we got to talking about politics. Once again I found that the conversation of two intelligent men must inevitably turn to politics, to political matters, to the absolute necessity of clear reason. Here, the high intelligence of my companion became all the more evident.'

Obvious, I thought, a Frenchman talking!

(What he had to say about democracy had made a great impression on my uncle, who is a perfect listener.)

'The Frenchman knew what democracy is,' said my uncle, 'what the state is today, young people above all and the state, the future and the state.'

'Precision,' said my uncle, 'distinguished the Frenchman, an elegant precision.'

The young Frenchman, related my uncle, was masterly in illuminating even the most sombre continuities not only of European politics but of world politics as a whole. Without even once quoting *from works of historical scholarship*, he was able in a couple of sentences to so clarify *the present-day historical view* that it *inevitably* elicited my uncle's admiration.

'You are a product of a school which doesn't really exist and nevertheless is the best there is,' my uncle had said to the young man.

The pair had walked as far as the oaks.

'I suggested to the Frenchman, that he eat supper with us,' said my uncle, 'but the Frenchman declined my invitation. He asked me to accompany him out of the forest, because he had lost his bearings, and I accompanied him out,' said my uncle. Then: 'The thought that I have perhaps seen this man for the last time is a painful one.'

On the way back through the mixed forest the Frenchman seemed to him to be 'one of the most important people' in his life. ('This man is altogether privileged,' said my uncle, 'as it is a privilege to meet such a man.')

23rd Sept.

Today I heard talk of a dead man 'shot through the head'.

25th Sept.

'The man concerned is an attaché at the French Embassy,' said my uncle.

the crime of an innsbruck

shopkeeper's Son

Even after a brief acquaintance with him I had extremely revealing insights into his development, into his childhood above all: sounds, smells in his parents' home, now many years behind him, he described to me again and again, the eeriness of a shopkeeper's gloomy house; his mother and the grocery-stillness and the birds trapped in the darkness in the high vaulting; the behaviour of his father, who in the shopkeeper's house in Anichstrasse constantly gave the orders of a ruthless master of properties and people. Georg always talked of his sisters' lies and slanders, of the devilish tricks with which siblings can often proceed against siblings; sisters have a criminal craving to destroy brothers, brothers to destroy sisters, brothers to destroy brothers and sisters to destroy sisters. His parents' house had never been a house of children, as are most of the other houses, parents' houses, especially in better areas, better atmospheric conditions, but a terrible adults' house, furthermore a huge and damp one, in which children have never come to the world, but right away dreadful arithmeticians, big-mouth infants with a nose for business and for the suppression of altruism.

Georg was an exception. He was the centre of attention, but thanks to his worthlessness, thanks to the scandal which he represented for the whole family, always frightened and embittered by him, not least where they tried to cover it up, a horribly crooked and crippled centre of attention, which they wanted out of the house at all costs. He was so greatly and in the most

dreadful way deformed by nature that they always had to hide him. After they had been disap-
pointed down to the depths of their faecal and
victual detestableness by the doctors' skills and
by medical science altogether, they implored in
mutual perfidiousness a fatal illness for Georg,
which would remove him from the world as
swiftly as possible; they had been prepared to do
anything, if he would just die; but he didn't die
and, although all of them together have done
everything to make him fall fatally ill, he did not
once fall *dangerously* ill (neither in Innsbruck,
where, separated by the River Inn, he had grown
up a couple of hundred yards away from me—
neither knew of the other—nor later, during our
Viennese studies in a room on the third floor of a
house in Zirkusgasse); among them he had only
grown larger and larger and ever more ugly and
frail, ever more worthless and in need of help,
but without his organs being affected, which
functioned better than their own . . . This develop-

ment on Georg's part embittered them, above all, because at the very moment at which he had been thrown by his screaming mother onto a corner-stone of the washhouse floor, they had come to the decision to revenge themselves in their way for the horrible surprise of the birth of an initially huge, damp and fat, but then, even if ever larger, then ever more delicate and healthy unsightly 'cripple son' (as his father called him), and to com-pensate themselves for an injustice that cried to heaven; like conspirators, they had decided to get rid of him, of Georg, and without coming into conflict with the law, even before he, as they rumi-nated, could deal them a possibly fatal injury through his mere existence; for years they believed that the point in time at which they would no longer have to put up with him was close, but they were deceived, had deceived themselves, his health, his lack of illness—as far as Georg's lungs, Georg's heart, all the other important organs were concerned—were stronger than their will and their shrewdness.

In part dismayed, in part megalomaniac, they
noted, as he rapidly grew larger and healthier
and more delicate and more intelligent and more
ugly, that he, they really believed so, had not
come out of their centuries' old merchants' substance and had remained stuck at home with
them; after several still-births, they had presumably deserved one of their own, a straight—not
crooked—piece of timber of merchant stock,
who should support them one and all right from
the very first moment, then later carry, raise even
higher one and all, raise parents and sisters even
higher *up*, than they already were; and what they
got, where from seemed strange to them, because
ultimately nevertheless by the father out of the
mother, was a creature that, as they saw it, had
been such a useless, ever deeper and deeper
thinking beast, that even had a claim to clothing
and to entertainment, and that one was supposed
to support it instead of being supported, feed instead of being fed, pamper instead of being pam-
pered; on the contrary, in his complete

uselessness Georg was and perpetually remained
a lump of flesh that was constantly in their way
and lay heavily in their stomachs and who even
wrote poems. Everything about him was different; they felt him to be the greatest disgrace in
their family otherwise composed solely of reality
and not in the least out of imagination. In the
room in the Zirkusgasse in Vienna which we had
rented after meeting in an inn in the Leopold-
stadt district and joining forces, he talked again
and again of his 'child's dungeon at Innsbruck',
and he flinched in front of his listener, in front of
me, who for years, for eight semesters, was his
only listener, when he thought he had to utter the
always, for him, difficult word, 'horsewhipping'.
Cellars and hallway and attic stores far too big,
far too huge for him, stone steps far too high for
him, trapdoors that were too heavy, jackets and
trousers and shirts (his father's worn-out jackets
and trousers and shirts) far too wide for him,
whistles from his father, screams from his mother

that were too shrill, the sniggering of his sisters, leaps by rats, the barking of dogs, cold and hunger, narrow-minded loneliness, schoolbags that were far too heavy for him, loaves of bread, sacks of Indian corn, sacks of flour, sacks of sugar, sacks of potatoes, shovels and steel wheelbarrows, incomprehensible instructions, tasks, threats and orders, punishments and chastisements, strokes and blows made up his childhood. Years after he had left home, he was still tormented by the cured sides of pork lugged by him down to the cellar and again lugged up out of the cellar (and lugged by him with what terrible pain). Even years later and four hundred and fifty miles away, in Vienna, he still anxiously crossed, head down, the parental Innsbruck shopkeeper's yard, descended, shaken by fever, to the parental Innsbruck shopkeeper's cellar. When, cuffed day in day out into the parental commercial arithmetic, he made a mistake, he was (not yet six the first time) locked into the cellar vault by his father or by his mother or by one of his sisters, and then for a while called only 'criminal'; at first, only his father had called him a criminal, but later, as he remembered, his sisters, too, then even his mother had joined in. Completely 'incapable of bringing up a child', she, whom he now imagined, after years, in his time as a student in Vienna, he saw in a mellower light, because he was separated from her by many mountains, always completely yielded, when it came to Georg, to the stronger side of the family, that is, to his father and his sisters. With shocking regularity, father and mother had beaten him several times a week with the whip.

In his childhood, the sons screamed in the houses of the Innsbruck shopkeepers, as did the pigs in the houses of the Innsbruck butchers. In his home, everything had no doubt been worse. His birth, so they assured him at every opportunity, had lead to their ruin. His father had constantly described him as 'unconstitutional', his father incessantly needled him with the word 'unconstitutional'. His sisters took advantage of him for their plots, using their sharpening minds with ever greater perfection. He was everyone's victim. When I saw into his childhood and into his Innsbruck, I saw into my childhood and my Innsbruck, with how much dismay simultaneously into my own, which had been dominated not by the same dreadfulness but by an even greater infamy, for my parents did not act out of bestial violence, as his did, but out of a radical philosophical violence coming from the head and from nowhere but the head and from heads.

Every day, early in the morning, an embitterment, saddening, deeper than by nature admissible, thrust our painful, incompetent heads together into one whole, hopeless, dull state of conjecture: everything in us and on us and about us suggested that we were lost, I just as much as he, whatever we had to look at and whatever we had to work out, whatever we had to walk and

stand and sleep and dream, whatever it had to do
with. For days Georg was often in the most re-
mote Higher Imagination, as he called it, and at
the same time he always walked, as I was continually forced to observe, back and forth in his des-
perations, which also overshadowed me, from a
certain point in time we, both the laws and their
makers, and the day-in–day-out coarse annihila-
tors of every law, all at once went together and as
if together forever through the whole great
pathological schema of colours, in which nature
had to express itself in each one of us as the most
painful of all human pains. For years we lodged,
even if on the surface of the capital, then nevertheless in a system of protective conduits created
by us for us and only visible to us; but in these
conduits we also uninterruptedly breathed in a
deadly air; we walked and we crawled almost entirely only in these conduits of our youthful despair and youthful philosophy and youthful
science always towards ourselves . . . these con-

duits led us out of our Zirkusgasse room, in which we sat in our chairs at the table, usually stricken by the power of judgement and by the monstrous excess of history, stricken by ourselves, over our books, dreadful bunglings, adulations and mockeries of our own and the whole geological genealogy, into the old, ancient body of the city and back out of it again to our room . . . Georg and I spent eight dreadful semesters together, had to spend them together, in this way that I've only hinted at, in the Zirkusgasse room; no pause of any kind had been permitted us; in all the eight semesters, in which I had sickened myself of jurisprudence, Georg no less of his pharmacy, we had not been capable of raising ourselves from our stooped posture, from both our deformities (I, too, had already been deformed), because, of course, as already indicated, we had always, in everything and everyone, to move in our conduits and hence stooped low, not capable of raising ourselves from this neces-

sity into a less bent one, no matter by how little;
in all the eight semesters we had not once had the
strength to get up and leave . . . We had not even
had the strength, because we didn't feel like it, to
open the window of our Zirkusgasse room and
let in fresh air . . . still less had we had just one of
the *invisible powers* . . . Our disposition, like our
mind, had been so firmly sealed up that by
human standards we should one day have suffo-
cated in ourselves, we were not so far away from
it, had not something that did not come from us,
could not come *from one of us*, such a metaphys-
ical intervention from outside in us or from deep
inside us, produced an alteration in our condition
out of two like conditions, Georg's and mine . . .
In the course of tremendously complicated pro-
ceedings against us, in the atmosphere of the capital, which to us remained atonic, our souls also
shrunk together. As so many of our age we were
without backing, had been deeply dug and deeply
buried into the idea that says that there is

nowhere, neither inside nor out, a possibility of fresh air and what it can produce, *unleash* or *efface*, and, indeed, for us in the Zirkusgasse room there was no fresh air; eight semesters long no fresh air.

We each of us had a name, one of many, which had come into existence in the mountains, many generations ago, one left of the Inn, one right of the Inn, countless generations in his case, had grown ever larger, but which now, as a destroyer of ourselves, at the end of parental curses and feats of arithmetical skill, had been transplanted to the shamelessly, as we were forced to see, self-pityingly decaying capital. Each of us was enclosed in his significant name and could not get out again. Neither knew the dungeon of the other, the guilt, the crime of the other, but each *suspected* that the other's dungeon and the other's guilt and crime were his own. Our mistrust for each other and of each other had over time increased in the same measure as we more and more belonged together, did not want to leave each other. Yet we hated each other, and we were the most opposite creatures one can imagine; everything of one shone from the other, indeed *out of the other*, but the two of us did not resemble each other in any way or any thing, in no sentiment at all, in nothing. And yet either of us could have been the other, everything of one could have come from the other . . . I often told myself, that I *could* be Georg, everything that Georg was, that meant, however, that nothing of Georg was *from* me . . . How other students, when they have been sent to the capital, enthusiastically find pleasure and refreshment in its possibilities of distraction, remained a mystery to us, nothing aroused our enthusiasm, nothing found favour with us, the spirit of the capital was a dead one, its entertainment apparatus too primitive for us.

From the beginning, we, he and I, operated with keen perception, in almost every case we subjected everything to our deadly criticism;

finally, our attempts to break out failed, everything weighed on us, we fell ill, we constructed
our conduit system. Already in our first weeks
we had withdrawn from the silent megalomania
of Vienna, from the city in which there was no
longer any history, any art and any scholarship,
in which there was no longer anything. But even
before my arrival in Vienna, still on the train, I
(as he also), we had both, independently of each
other, been attacked by an illness, by a fever
gradually making us sad, I by a *distraction to the
point of fatal over-sensitivity*, moving logically
from everything external into myself, in my sub-
conscious just as in full consciousness and, sitting
in one of our many dark express train compart-
ments, which are drawn through the land at high
speed, in awareness of myself and in awareness
of what went with me always, was surprised by
the first thoughts of suicide, the signs of suicide,
for a long time. With what a grey and extraordi-
narily severe gloominess did I all at once have to

cope with between the Melk Hills! On this jour-
ney, which I had been forced to make against my
will, I had several times wished for my death,
swift, sudden, painless, of which only a picture of
peace is left behind; especially on the dangerous
curves, as close by the Danube at Ybbs. The jour-
ney of young people from the provinces to the
capital in order to begin a feared course of studies, for a course of studies which most of them
don't want, almost always proceeds to the accom-
paniment of the most dreadful state in the brain
and mind and emotions of the person concerned
and deceived and hence tortured. The thought of
suicide in one apprehensively, and in all cases always less boldly than expected, approaching at
twilight by train a secondary school or college or
university in the capital, is most natural. How
many and not a few whom I knew and with
whom I grew up and who have been mentioned
to me by name have already thrown themselves
from the moving train shortly after taking leave of

their parents at their local station . . . As far as Georg and I are concerned, we never revealed our suicide perspectives to each other, we only knew of each other that we were at home in them. We were enclosed in our thoughts of suicide as in our room and in our conduit system, as in a complicated game, comparable to advanced mathematics. In this advanced suicide game we often left each other completely in peace for weeks. We studied and thought about suicide; we read and thought about suicide; we hid away and slept and dreamed and thought about suicide. We felt abandoned in our thoughts of suicide, undisturbed; no one bothered about us. We were at liberty to kill ourselves at any time, but we did not. As much as we had always been strangers to each other, there were never any of the many hundreds of thousands of odourless human secrets between us, only the secret of nature *as such*, which we knew about. Days and nights were like verses of an infinitely harmonious dark song to us.

On the one hand, his family had already
known from the start that he was unsuitable for
his father's business profession and so for taking
over the shop on Anichstrasse which demanded
someone like them, on the other hand they were
far from giving up hope that Georg, the cripple,
could become, almost overnight, possibly from
one blow of the whip to the next, what they from
the start wanted him to be: the successor to the
grocer who was now already in his sixties!
Finally, however, they had decided, as if by agree-
ment, behind his, Georg's back, overnight, for
always, in favour of his older sister, and from
that moment on they stuffed, whatever way they
could, everything that they could, all their shopkeepers' powers and all their shopkeepers'
knowledge into fat, ruddy, rustic Irma, a person
who on her fat legs walked all day long through
the shopkeeper's house like a heavy cow; summer
as winter in puffed sleeves, she, who was just
twenty and engaged to a butcher's assistant from

Natters, her calves constantly discharging pus,
grew into a pillar of the shop. At the same moment at which they had decided on the sister as
successor (no doubt also in view of her fiancé!),
they consented to Georg going to university.
They had been afraid of losing face. But they
didn't permit him, as he had wished, to study
pharmacy in Innsbruck, where, in addition to the
commercial apprenticeship, he had completed the
grammar school with a good record, or in nearby
Munich, but only in distant Vienna far to the
east, which he and all of them had always hated.
They wanted him as far away from themselves as
possible, to *know* him far away, and the capital
really was at the end of the world. Every young
person today knows what an exile there means!
It had made no difference that he had tried to
make clear to them that Vienna, the capital, had
for decades been the most backward of all European university towns; there was no course of
study in Vienna that could be recommended; he

had to go to Vienna and, if he did not want to
make do with the lowest of all allowances known
to me, he had to remain in Vienna, the most
dreadful of all old cities of Europe. Vienna is
such an old and lifeless city, is *such* a cemetery,
left alone and abandoned by all of Europe and all
of the world, we thought, what a vast cemetery
of crumbling and premodern curiosities!

As if he had been me, that's what I always felt
in the last period when we were together, and with
especial intensity towards the end of the year
when, before falling asleep, he hinted at everything of which we knew nothing at all . . . His inability, just once in his life to make himself
intelligible, was also mine . . . His childhood,
which had appeared to him endless, not a thousand years long, like that of the author of *Moby
Dick*: the uninterruptedly vain attempt to win the
confidence of his parents and of the other people
around him, at least of those closest to him. He
had never had a real friend—but who knows what

that is—only people who made fun of him, secretly feared him; he was always someone, who disturbed the harmony of another or several others in his way, through his deformity, he was continually disturbing . . . Wherever he went, wherever he stayed, he was an ugly spot of colour on the beautiful calm background . . . People were only there (he thought) to set traps for him, no matter who or what they were, what they represented, there was nothing that did not set a trap for him, not even religion. Finally, he was darkened by his own feeling . . . His awakening had no doubt also been one into the madness of hopelessness . . . He had all at once, and I had already felt safe, torn open the door to my childhood with the brutality of the sick, oppressed, despairing . . . Every morning, he woke up in the firmly locked cell of a new age-old day.

Whereas for me, figures which are easily recognized as comic, indeed even as playful, again and again appeared in front of the gloomy backdrop of my childhood, something like that never happened to my friend; when he looked into the past, only terrifying occurrences were visible to him, and what had been put on there and was still being put on there was even more terrifying; he wanted, therefore, he said repeatedly, to look as little as ever he could, not look at all into the past, which was like the present and the future, which *was* present and future, not look at all; but that wasn't possible; his childhood, his youth, his whole life had been a vast ice-cold stage, only there to terrify him, and the leading roles on this stage were always only taken by his parents and his sisters; again and again, they invented something new to upset him. Sometimes he wept, and when I asked him why, he replied: because he couldn't draw the stage curtain; he was too weak to do it; less and less often was he able to draw the stage curtain, he was afraid that one day he would be unable to draw it all; wherever he went, wherever he found himself, in whatever

condition he was, he was forced to watch his
play; the most terrible scenes took place again
and again in his parents' house in Innsbruck, in
the shopkeeper's house; father and mother as
driving forces of its deadly scenery, he always
saw and heard them. Often, in his sleep, he said
the words 'father' and 'mother' and the words
'whip' and 'cellar' or a 'No no!' finally hunted to
death by one of his persecutors, which was to do
with his many chastisements. In the early morning, his body, crippled, yet refined to the point of
a chastity forbidden to nature (he had the skin of
mortally ill girls), was wet, a fever, which
couldn't be measured, already weakened him before he had even got up. We usually did not eat
breakfast, because eating and drinking disgusted
us. The lectures disgusted us. The books disgusted us. The world to us was a perverse bestial
and perverse philosophical plague and repulsive
operetta. During the last February, Georg had
been constantly sad and, in his sadness, always

alone. He, who was one year younger, was forced
to be afraid in the evenings under the conditions
known to both of us, supported by hand movements, movements of his head, among all the
names of deceased or of still living creatures and
objects feared by him. The letters addressed to
him, the few, contained, like those to me, only
admonitions to recovery, nothing good-natured.
Once he had pronounced the word 'tactless', he
had meant the world was at least tactless. How
different we both would have had to be, to turn
our backs on this cemetery, which the capital had
been, which the capital *is*. We were too weak to
do it. In the capital, everyone is too weak. 'This
city is a cemetery which is dying out!' is the last
thing he had said; after this statement, which did
not give me pause for thought, at first, which had
the same standing as all the rest by him recently, I
had, it was the fourteenth, half past ten in the
evening, gone to bed. When I was woken, just
before two by a noise, because Georg had been

completely still, probably not least for the one reason, that under no circumstances did he want to wake me up (and now I know how agonizing that must have been for him), I made the dreadful discovery, which Georg's parents now describe as their son's crime against himself and against his family. Georg's father had already arrived in Vienna from Innsbruck at ten the next morning and requested that I throw light on the matter. When I had returned from the hospital to which Georg had been taken, Georg's father was already in our room, and I knew, even though it had still been dark because of the bad weather, there was no further change that day, that the man packing Georg's things was his father. Although also from Innsbruck, I had never seen him before. Once, however, my eyes had got used to the darkness and were also able to take advantage of the darkness, and I shall never forget this keenness of my eyes, I saw that this man, who was wearing a black coat with a sheepskin lining, that this man, who gave the impression of being in a hurry and was throwing everything of Georg's onto a heap, in order to remove it, that this man and that everything connected to him bore the blame for Georg's misfortune, for the catastrophe.

the carPenTeR

Someone, as in the case of the carpenter Winkler,
released from prison with a shocking suddenness,
is, as I am forced again and again to conclude,
impossible to help. Winkler, about whom the
newspapers five years ago, for the duration of his
trial, wrote an unbelievable amount that was vul-
gar and repellent, at the weekends with pictures
of his victim and of himself, from the trial and
from the scene of the crime, was in Ischl on 25
October. His sister, who works at the tannery in
Vöklabruck, called on me on the afternoon of the

twenty-fifth and requested me to see Winkler, who was waiting outside, let him into the building for a few minutes; he needed to talk to me, inform me of various things regarding himself, both agreeable and disagreeable, more disagreeable than agreeable. Only just released, he wanted to thank me, because the fact that he only had to serve five out of seven years was my doing alone. Furthermore, I, who had been assigned to him five years ago to prepare the case and to defend him, was the only person whom he was not afraid to confide in now that he was out of Garsten. All others he was afraid of, on the other hand all others were afraid of him. His earlier acquaintances in particular now avoided talking to Winkler, they shied away from the least contact with him. No one greeted him, no one allowed themselves to be greeted by him. Not a soul had a word to say to him. But about him they had quite shocking words to say. For the most part they behaved as though he didn't exist. He himself didn't dare address anyone. Lies continued to be spread about him—all Ischl was talking about him and his unworthiness. Slanders were doing the rounds; it hurt him constantly; she, his sister, only hoped that her brother would not act on all these terrible things. Everything was being made difficult for him in the vilest way. She had no illusions at all, she saw the occurrences hurting her brother quite clearly. The village and its surroundings were a constant source of quite unjustified spite against him. When she came to Ischl, then she, who was not in the least to blame, was also affected. She did not believe that a human being could bear such a state of affairs, she could not imagine that he would go on living in an area which continued to undermine him with every refinement. Winkler's sister, as she stood in front of me in my chambers at about five in the afternoon, made a desperate impression on me. She expected, she said, nothing from her brother except blows, reproaches,

outer and inner hurts. His character was un-
changed, and both she and I were familiar with
it. Throughout her life, throughout her childhood
and youth, above all during the most important
time when she was growing up, she had been
forced to suffer because of Winkler's 'terrifying'
character, everyone around him, parents, grandparents, had always been oppressed by him. The
brutality of his sudden appearances and interven-
tions in the family, in peace and order, his 'de-
structive urge' had always cowed everyone.
Parents and grandparents and neighbours had
been constantly afraid of him, fear gripping every
limb, she herself had the whole time had dealings
with the court because of him and finally been
ruined by him for good. She also blamed him for
the early death of her parents. She mentioned
many examples of his unbelievable physical brutality, repeatedly she referred, in everything that
she now hastily expressed, to his nature, fused
into one big misfortune. 'From his stupid head'

he had dominated everything around him, often hit out from top to bottom; only they, parents and sister, had always hushed everything up. Bigger injuries, however, had become known to the country police, and, again and again, at ever shorter intervals, he had been imprisoned, removed from them, for ever longer periods. Yet she had always loved her brother, she still had affection for her brother, which she couldn't explain. Often, at home, he would, for days, have been in the most good-natured mood, but then, in a flash, turned into the beast, as which he often appeared to her at night. But she could say 'nothing good at all' about her now thirty-five year-old brother, when she considers, when she has to look in her memory, she would have to remain silent as to how he constantly treated her in the vilest way and already as a two-year-younger, utterly defenceless schoolgirl, always *mis*treated her, over the years ever more roughly with his uninterruptedly 'terrible physical and mental

development', ever more 'monstrously'; she dare
not think about their schooldays together, their
time together as apprentices, the time in which
she went to the tannery, he to the carpenter's
shop. In his irresponsible state, he had surprised
her and inflicted on her a series of physical and
mental injuries, in part affecting her whole life.
Because of his threats against her she had remained, for a large part of her childhood and
youth, noticeably quiet towards her whole surroundings. If she only thought of 'the night behind the station' ('The time at the saltworks')—I
stopped her from having to explain herself in detail—it was incomprehensible to her that she was
now ('but perhaps out of fear of him?') speaking
up for him, after he had 'systematically smashed'
her life. ('He ruined us all!') It seemed altogether
strange to her, that she was now standing in front
of me to plead for her brother; but she was
pleading 'urgently', that now, 'when he is so
abandoned', I should not turn him away. She had
only come up to see me first to announce him, as

a precaution; in just under an hour, she had to catch the post bus back to Vöklabruck where she had been employed 'for four years now', because, after Winkler's crime, his arrest and finally sentencing, there had been 'nothing more for her, no more life for her' in Ischl. I enquired whether she made a decent living in Vöklabruck and she said yes. Because of acts of violence by Winkler, which took place more than ten years ago, it was impossible for her to have a child. She only hinted at that, however, it was something I found very disturbing. Every evening in recent days, he, whose early release from Garsten had been a surprise ('an unpleasant one!') even to him, had waited outside the tannery to collect her. She had been unable to bear the sight of her brother who, 'dirty and repulsive,' had been walking up and down in front of the tannery before five every day. 'How ashamed I was,' she said. Without money ('He drank everything he had saved up!') he had suddenly, without warning, 'no card, nothing', suddenly turned up on her doorstep.

She lived outside Vöklabruck, 'on the Trench' she
said, as if that should mean something to me. 'He
could have written often,' she said, but he didn't
write. She talked of an escape attempt, of a plot
in the prison, which he, however, had not joined,
that had accelerated his release. She would not
have let him into her room if she had not been
afraid, 'he didn't come alone, there were two of
them', she said; but the second had disappeared
again immediately and not turned up again. Winkler had always, 'even as a child, had his foot in
the door'. They had been able to get along with
one another for a couple of days, then he had
begun to blame her—she wasn't doing anything
for him. At night she hadn't slept at all, only
'been on her guard'. He had only sat on the floor
all the time, 'crouching' she said, had also for a
long time often lain stretched out on the floor beside her bed, so that he had been able to brace
himself with head and feet between the walls.
Mostly, he had spent hours looking at the wall or

at her, his sister, and hardly eaten anything. He had also, except when he picked her up from the tannery, not gone out. 'All the time' she had bought him something to drink, not much, but 'far too much'. His smell, the smell, which all her life she had been afraid of, was now in her room, and she would never get this smell out of her room again. She had often been unable to stand any more with tiredness, but he ruthlessly made her go to various inns for various spirits. From the moment at which her brother had settled in-with her, she had not slept any more. 'His big hands, Herr Doktor!' she said. Being with him, and then when she had been in the tannery, the thought of him had been very troubling for her. Soon, she no longer had any idea about how she could free herself from her brother again. 'That was bad.' In prison, Winkler, in her opinion, had got worse. She had been most afraid of the im-mobility with which he had constantly 'crouched' on the floor. 'Such a strong man,' she said. She

had, 'out of calculation', as she expanded on
what she said, repeatedly wanted to start a conversation with him, to distract both of them, but
he had never said one word more than absolutely
necessary, even food and drink and pieces of
clothing he had ordered her to give him only
with gestures of the hand, 'brief, abrupt'. Because
she had to buy him a suit and a coat, shoes, un-
derpants ('I didn't do it unwillingly!'), her savings had been gone in a couple of days. Suddenly,
perhaps half an hour had passed, she said: 'I
hope he's still downstairs!' She wanted, I could
see that, to go to the window, but didn't have the
courage to do so. What would become of her
brother, who was 'so big and so silent', she said,
but without then saying another word apart from
'so big and so silent', she turned round and ran,
as if finally she wanted to hide herself completely
in her coat, down to the hall, with such awkward
movements of her legs, which suggest an injustice
inflicted on the creature they had to bear. I no

longer heard, although I should have heard it, because the door of the chambers had been open
and everything said in the hall, no matter how
softly can be heard clearly up in the chambers,
what she had said to Winkler in passing, I heard
nothing more except the street door slamming
shut, which for years has always startled me and
is ever more repellent. Shortly after that Winkler
appeared in my room.

He made the same impression of strength on
me as on his sister. It struck me that his face had
coarsened during the long period of imprisonment; the dangerous look in his eyes gave me
pause for thought. His hands were restless, and
he emanated an unbelievable unease, which
alarmed me. In part he had come through the
door like a child, in part like an over-mature
man, entering so suddenly that I assumed he had
been listening behind the door while I was con-
versing with his sister. But then nothing had been
mentioned by his sister and myself which would

not also have been meant for him. I was indeed
alarmed at the thought that Winkler had been listening behind the door, had come into the house
and up the stairs behind his sister unnoticed; on
the other hand, his breathlessness indicated a
rapid ascent of the stairs. He wanted to, but
could not speak. On the whole, he seemed to be
glad that his sister had seen me before him. His
coat was too tight, his shirt collar was unbut-
toned; this man has a pathological attitude towards everything and everyone, I thought. I
remember that he had been more helpless than
permissible in court, above all at the crucial moments, and I was now once again won over by
the same helplessness. There was certainly not, at
the moments he came into my chambers, nor
later, or the whole time he was with me, the least
lack of feeling between him and me. Only the
possibilities of communication on either side
were painfully limited. During the conversation
with his sister, I had no longer been able to re-

member what he looked like. He came from a
breed of people whose substance quite lacked
awareness. He had one of those faces that one
often sees at evening in our villages when, tired
oneself, one walks through the weariness of silent
groups of people, who are no longer capable of
protest of any kind, through the chained physiog-
nomies of the labouring country folk. Winkler
had been quite indistinct to me, as I now realized, when his sister had been talking to me
about him, a different man from the one now
standing before me. I had only heard his voice
even before he had come in and said a single
word; voices stick in my mind once and for all.
His manner of speaking, like that of all the sub-
ordinated, excluded, was awkward, like a body
full of wounds into which at any time anyone
can strew salt, yet so insistent that it is painful to
listen to it. He had come to thank me, for what, I
already knew. I had got 'the best' I could out of it
for him. The court and the time, when his crime

had taken place, had been hostile to him from the start; a court should be different; but he said neither the word 'unbiased' nor the word 'objective'. He immediately reminded me of my visits to his cell when he was on remand. Much of what he reminded me in connection with my efforts on his behalf, which had been no more than duty, I had already long forgotten; he had remembered in their entirety whole sentences I had said to him five years ago. Winkler's attachment, which became clear to me from everything he said and didn't say, dismayed me. All in all, it seemed to me both exaggerated and dangerous. Again and again, he said I had been 'useful' to him. It was as if in all the five years he had at all times remained in contact with me. I myself had already forgotten Winkler the moment he had been led out of the courtroom—a lawyer finishes with a client's case shortly after the guilty verdict; I remembered: out on the street the Winkler case was no longer on my mind . . . Over the

years he had wanted to write to me, but again
and again he had shrunk back from doing so. 'I
am a stupid man,' he said; several times he said:
'I am a stupid man.' I invited him to take a seat.
He sat down opposite me; I moved the lamp to
the middle of the desk, but then away again and
finally switched it off altogether, because he
didn't want any light and we could see well
enough without it. I don't like any half-light
either. It's good that the desk is between him and
me, I thought, then he began, looking at the
floor, to talk for a long time about particular ex-
periences in prison, finally about the monotony
and about the complete absence of surprise there.
He talked and mused and talked again. I knew
everything, he thought. As with everything, one
can also, as far as prison and its laws and lack of
laws are concerned, be for and against them.
Time had grown longer for him from day to day.
He complained about the warders, not about the
food. From his cell he had been able to look into

a wood, sometimes also beyond the wood to a mountain chain. The torment of being unable to cope with time was greatest in unfreedom, in penal institutions and prisons. He had worked in the carpenter's shop. There had been no question of privileges for him—he had always forfeited all of them. His ability to make do with a minimum of space, as one must do in a prison cell, for a long time with his own body, nothing else, had been of advantage to him. 'But all the things one sees!' he said. He remembered the moment sentence was pronounced, the silence in the court while outside it had begun to snow. That detail I had completely forgotten. As for himself, the Garsten warders had not indulged in any physical punishments, but nor in all the five years had he been violent. 'Justice and injustice,' he said, a man like him has a lot to think about there, less to say. As for Garsten Prison, there were a number of noteworthy peculiarities which he informed me about. I asked him what he was

thinking of doing now. Although I knew it was
out of the question, I asked whether he had already looked for a job, and then I said he should
see to it as quickly as possible 'and with determi-
nation'. It wasn't hard for a carpenter to find a
job. He was good at his trade. 'They're building
everywhere,' I said, 'the fewer craftsmen there
are, the better for each individual one.' But what
I said, possibly in a much too patronizing tone,
made no impression whatsoever on him. I suddenly asked myself whether the man was not
lost. He said, for him everything was already too
late, there was nothing any more, that it was
worth his while starting out on. 'Nothing. Nothing,' he said. Also nothing on which he still had a
claim. He had long ago 'forfeited' all claims. He
spoke the insipid big city word without expression, yet it sounded mystical and shook me. Even
the thought of having to rise from his chair again
gave him the headache from which he had already been suffering for years. Impossible, once

again in his life, that was also 'mucked up', to present himself to one of the employers, master carpenters or builders. 'All much too late,' he said. Up to that moment I had not had a proper idea of the seriousness of the whole, sad as well as strange, situation, and I guided what I said, quite consciously, in a direction, to a word, which he found unpleasant: I now said again and again only: 'work!' But then I recognized the foolishness of my action and desisted. His argument—that in Ischl, where everyone knew everything about everyone, he would not find any work, and he didn't want to go anywhere else— was of course based on an error, but I did not contradict him; it seemed to me that I had to let him be. He knew that he could not return to his sister again, but on the other hand . . . then again: his biggest mistake had been to seek shelter, comfort with her, 'and she has nothing herself'. Again and again, he said how very afraid of him she was: 'of me!' he exclaimed. He said: 'Go

where? Vöklabruck was closest . . .' The accusation, that within a couple of days he had taken
all his sister's money, 'without consideration', I
said, he did not accept; she would get back what
he owed her. I knew, I said, that he had threatened her every day. There was now a commotion
on the street which I deliberately ignored. I
would, I said, try to quickly obtain a job for him.
A good worker—Winkler was one, I said, even if
he was called Winkler and even in the town of
Ischl, had nothing to fear; on the contrary, anyone would welcome him with open arms. 'People,' I said, 'only look at your hands.' I offered
him what seemed to me appropriate financial
support for the coming night; it would be particularly cold, I said, and he must get a good sleep;
he refused, however, to accept money from me.
In a couple of days he would have found work
and accommodation, I said. I did not want to
give up, that's what I said to myself: don't give
up! Perhaps he would be employed tomorrow,

then he would be earning money and he could
pay back every debt, and things would be looking up, very quickly looking up. He should get a
good sleep and come back again with a clear
head; I would always be at his disposal. He
didn't listen. He looked at the corn cob, which,
because I like it, I had lying on the window-sill.
As if the five long-drawn-out years in prison had
convinced him of the pointlessness of even the
least, the most inconspicuous, signs of life, he did
not respond at all to what I had said but suddenly asked, and the unconnectedness of the sentence he had spoken, which then lay for a long
time in the air between us, dismayed me: how
much money would one need, to travel so far
away, that no one would under any circumstances be affected any more . . . ? A pained burst
of laughter on my part must have deeply of-
fended him, because he fell silent and was for
several minutes completely motionless at this
clumsiness, which had been an act of indecency.

Cautiously, I then had him describe his birth-
place, a village in the Niedere Tauern Alps, which
he all at once embellished, fearlessly, it seemed to
me, with descriptions of his way to school, his
teachers, his parents and his sister. I was struck
by a liking on his part for crooked lanes, freshly
slaughtered meat; his attitude to the deceased, to
acts of political violence in the countryside; so-
cialism, political parties altogether he rejected.
One can place many traps for such a person, and
such a person will step into them. With great
conviction he suddenly talked again about the
most various sad incidents in his life, he painted,
the more these incidents appeared to draw closer
to his ultimately awful helplessness, only grey
pictures. Everything he said was of an even grey
or grey-black or black-grey dominated by his
strange misfortune. His voice was neither soft
nor loud, it did not really belong to him but
came from his conditions and contexts; at best, a
fundamental comparison could be drawn as if in

THOMAS BERNHARD

consideration of a not-yet-living and already-no-
longer living, but existing, creature which is yet
no mere object. He made what he said in the
condensed, suddenly complete afternoon silence
of the chambers, above all, because it was almost
dark, tremendously vivid. That afternoon, which
is unusual, and also that evening, I had no urgent
work to deal with, and I was glad not to have to
leave the building any more, and so I left it up to
Winkler to leave or to stay. For a moment it
seemed to me as if he had only wanted to warm
up in my chambers. His sister was surely long
ago back in Vöklabruck. I thought: the childless-
ness of two people like the Winkler siblings,
which has in each of them for whatever reason
become an irreversible permanent state, can lead
to the highest and most dizzying heights and
down to horrible powerlessness. I asked him
whether he had already eaten supper, the people
in the Upper Austrian countryside always eat
their supper early, although I knew that his stom-

ach was empty; no doubt he had not eaten anything either at midday, because then brother and
sister had been hurrying from Vöklabruck to the
town of Ischl on the post bus—that too a cause
of his tiredness. He declined to eat something
with me, 'something warm', I had said, which
could have been found in the kitchen attached to
the chambers. Nor did he want anything to
drink. Basically this man, who on the one hand
was as much a stranger to me as anyone could
be, on the other was anything but a stranger,
dominated me. A criminal is undoubtedly a poor
soul, who is punished for his poverty. I thought
that far beyond the limit of even advanced science. He could, he said, for reasons he could not
explain, also because of 'lack of bearings', say
nothing about the especially gross incidents in
the prison, which he deliberately remained silent
about and which again and again occupied his
mind. He only felt everything and the consequences of that were fatal. An existence like his

was enfeebling; imprisonment ruined every useful feeling for the outside world in a man, it blocked access to it. Mending his ways, as had always been demanded of him, was not something someone like him could manage. He had no possibilities of reforming and improving himself, he had never had them. He didn't even want to reform. What does that mean? His childhood and his youth had been overshadowed by the hopelessness of ever being able to reform and improve himself. All the prerequisites of a life that proceeds inconspicuously and doesn't hurt anyone had always really been missing in his case. By disposition he had been from the outset nothing but a dark source of cruelties and pain. An upbringing which was completely wrong, because not even attempts at it were present had pushed his predispositions into and down to the criminal. His hurts, even the very earliest ones, had been dealt with unfeelingly, instead of in linen his parents had wrapped him in their physical and emotional coldness. Only with his physical strength, he had suddenly become aware of it, could he one day overcome familial oppression; he simply hit out if he was being annoyed. This method, the only one he knew to keep himself above water, to make himself heard, indeed even respected, within a short time led him to the prisons. Being imprisoned, he said, increased fear and antipathy. There existed today a highly developed administration of justice, but no progress in the administration of justice. Modern prison methods had their 'crafty' peculiarities. He said the words 'isolation hysteria', which he must have heard or read—they were not his own. Modern punishment no longer entered into the body of the convict, but exclusively now deep into his soul, it penetrated where once, fifty years ago, nothing had penetrated. He could not explain what he meant. The contemporary administration of justice functioned to disturb people, and I thought: as a science in itself. The sight of

his newly bought clothes again made me ask myself how Winkler could come into money as
quickly as possible. The danger that he entirely
cuts himself off from the outside world, had to
cut himself off, if he has not already cut himself
off from it, withdrawn from it, at the first contact with it, was too apparent for me to be able
to leave him to his own devices. I imagined how
the purchase of his clothes, which were an insult
to him—and perhaps he had only bought them
for my sake?—had proceeded in a shop in Vöklabruck that morning; how he, Winkler, no doubt
paid attention to his sister, yet then, as he was
trying them on, did not pay attention to her,
made terrible clothing purchase decisions, how
his sister had to put up with many of his words
of abuse (she would have seen that the coat was
too big at the shoulders, but then again on the
whole too tight); the sales assistants in the clothing store gathering in the coats department; Winkler's peremptory tone towards the pale-faced

stupid girls, then again his naïve-rural manliness,
showing off, capable of disconcerting every
woman and girl's heart. Again I ventured, because I knew him sufficiently distracted, to make
the suggestion: he should, just for one night, stay
in one of the comparatively well-appointed and
cheap small hotels along the Lower Traun and
the following day come to see me. I had time for
him, my work had now to my surprise come to
something of a standstill; indeed, I had the intention of inviting him for breakfast the next morning, but did not express this intention.
'Meanwhile,' I said, but what I said only irritated
him, 'I have a couple of addresses, a skilled
worker . . .' I fell silent and resolved, after Winkler was gone, to enquire at one or two carpenter's shops, whether they were interested in
Winkler. I didn't foresee any difficulty in finding
employment for him. He should not worry, I
said, and I discovered, if I was not entirely mistaken, that I was once again talking the whole

time to a person who, even if he was pretending
to do so, out of courtesy, was not listening to me
at all, whose thoughts were everywhere, only not
with me. Only his body is sitting there, I thought,
Winkler may be in my chambers, but his
thoughts are not in my chambers. On the first
nights after his release, he had at first, 'in a better
state', been unable to make up his mind to spend
the night at an inn, he had not ventured to approach any house, still less a human being, and
he had been dreadfully cold; he had simply found
it impossible to address anyone and so, all those
days and nights, he had wandered about almost
entirely in the open, if possible in the woods
where he could assume that no one would meet
him. In some woods there was warmth, he said,
in others not. Completely exhausted, he had then
nevertheless gone to an inn, around midnight—
'at that time they don't check so carefully,' he
said. Regardless of his money, he had now only
been concerned not to freeze any more. '*How* I

froze!' he said. A country fair steward from Lambach, whom he had met outside an inn in Stadl Paura, had pulled the last remaining half of his money from his coat when Winkler had nodded off, but he had been able to stop 'the fellow' at the last moment. He also talked about how lucky he had been to have several big newspapers with him, with which he was able to cover himself in a hollow near Wimsbach. The inns would no doubt have let him in to their warmth to drink, he thought, not to sleep; his appearance had been too shabby. He had been able to endure twelve days in this way, not a day more. Finally, without a penny, he had gone on foot, across meadows and through woods, and contrary to the quite natural reluctance on his part, to Vöklabruck, to his sister. She had been shocked at the sight of him, and had not wanted to let him into her room. He had gone away again and joined someone in a very similar state to his own; both of them had been forced by his sister back onto the many dreadful paths in the cold and darkness, finally again in several inns and then, on the advice of the other, who had been wearing mechanic's overalls and who remained completely unknown to Winkler, ('I didn't even make a note of his name!'), back to his sister again. She had, said the carpenter, from the start been afraid of him, the same fear as *before* his time in prison, this fear of him had not changed since her childhood, this very particular fear, connected only to him and his misfortune. She believed he would make her room untidy, her landlady could give her notice because of his sudden appearance. She had also feared for her job in the tannery. He had picked her up from the tannery every day at five; he himself described her work there as 'hard'. On the way home she had been ashamed of him, and the idea of providing him with a new set of clothes— what he was wearing was ten years old!—had originally even come from her. But when she realized, that if she bought him new

clothes she would lose all her savings, she wanted
to draw back. But it was too late: on the morning
of the twenty-fifth, shortly before the two of
them came to see me, Winkler forced her to hand
over the money and come to the clothes store.
She herself had spoken of a now slowly increas-
ing soiling of her person by Winkler. On the first
evening she had refused to let him sleep on the
floor beside her bed, but there was no other possibility. He had lain down next to her on the
floor 'like a dog'. As there was no blanket, he
had been forced to make do with a couple of old
editions of the 'Linz Popular Paper'. During the
first night together, neither of them had slept.
Wordlessly they brooded in the little room in the
attic of the house 'On the Trench'. Again I
thought, Winkler had become noticeably calm,
that his only hope was a job. But the difficulties
in making that clear to him had by this point already painfully increased. Even while the people
are in prison, the judicial administration should

find work and lodgings for them, otherwise the
men immediately come into conflict with the law
again; the fault lies with the state, the society; the
authorities provide the released prisoner with
nothing but the horror of sudden freedom, again
and again the cause of countless relapses by men
altogether capable of improvement. The authorities are thereby repeatedly responsible for this
same contemptible negligence. The legal author-
ity, by disregarding its duty of care to the most
unfortunate, is positively criminal. Only the judicial administration had already known, at least
two weeks before the date, about his early release. It should have obtained a job for him. So
the state again and again saddles itself with ills
which should be got rid off, can be got rid off. I
myself was completely surprised by Winkler's
sudden release, even though I too, about a year
ago petitioned the Ministry of Justice for his
'Early Release Before Term'. But such petitions
are obligatory and usually only lead to success in
cases involving docile prisoners, those who are

'not a public danger'. In my opinion, Winkler did not have the slightest prospect of early release; it is also quite inconsistent with his prison description, which I studied only recently. Such surprising releases lead without fail, in almost all cases to complications, usually to catastrophe. Apart from his sister, Winkler has no relatives any more. Possibly his release is related to the rebuilding work, begun in March, of the streetside wing at Garsten in which Winkler had been held. On such occasions, releases which had often not been planned at all, are implemented surprisingly quickly. I asked Winkler, who now made an especially downcast impression, to show consideration for his sister who appeared to me to be in decidedly poor health. She believed, he was now, after this conversation with me, going back to stay with her. He must not do that. That was what she was afraid of. In view of the already overstrained relationship between the two of them, I thought it better he remain in Ischl. The weather, I said, was also to blame for his awful

state, which seemed hopeless to him, the damp
and cold, dark day. Naturally, no matter what he
undertook now, he could not avoid exertions,
sacrifices. His crime, as one of hundreds and
thousands of juvenile crimes, was, I said, pardon-
able. The whole world was a world of the excluded, society as such did not exist, each person
was alone, no one had an advantage over the
rest. He only appeared to be listening to what I
was saying. For a long time he looked at the
clock on the wall, a present from my sister-in-
law. I would, of course, waive repayment of the
defence costs. The defence costs repayment stipu-
lated by law is an unjustifiably harsh provision.
All impediments would be cleared out of the way
for him, he could rely on that. I would exert myself on his behalf in various places. He was not
alone with his crime, I repeated, everybody committed crimes, big ones, but most crimes went
undetected, unrecognized, unpunished. Crimes
were symptoms of illness; nature unceasingly
produced every possible kind of crime, including

human crimes; nature crimes were by right.
Everything was always in nature and from nature, nature was by nature criminal. Because he
made such a wretched impression, I asked him,
whether he did not at the moment, as was possible, have the strength to take a look at his life,
with the whole world behind him and then before him, to examine his after all incredible development, he would find in it, that also was part
of the laws of nature, not only dark places. The
world was not only dreadful. Matter was tremendously precise and full of beauty. Irrespective of
place and time, the individual was all the time capable of the most astonishing discoveries for the
sake of which life was worth living. But Winkler
said nothing in reply, he responded to nothing.
He seemed more and more to be shutting himself
up in himself, and in a dreadful idea of himself.
'If,' I remarked, 'the walks that one takes,' and I
was thinking more of myself than of him as I said
it, 'no longer lead into the woods or to the river
or into the warm and pulsating shelter of a town

or to the human in general and back again, but
now only, even if into the woods and to the river
and into the town and to the human in general,
into darkness and into nothing but darkness,
then one is lost.' It was clear to me, that Winkler,
had he taken money, would have gone to the inn,
and not to sleep . . . and the next day he would
have been incapable of presenting himself to one
of the master carpenters. How weak the big man
was, the giant! If he were to jump up and beat
me to a pulp! The thugs and killers jump up
abruptly out of their terrible weakness. Winkler
reminded me of an animal, existing in several
animals simultaneously, both wild and tame, in
hostility, in the nature of hostility. I need not
have informed myself about his childhood: the
assistant carpenter's certificate had been a spring-
board, placed very high, more by his parents
than by him, from which height, which for his
kind was often unattainable, he threw himself
into the depths, the deepest depths. On that

evening which had grown so unexpectedly sad, I dispensed with going for a walk, as I usually do. Winkler said nothing more and remained motionless, his coat buttoned up; finally sitting in the chair with his hands in his coat pockets. His head was then, hidden from me behind my books, on his knees. I leafed through various documents, while Winkler, fallen asleep, as I ascertained, now made only a frightful impression. He was spreading the smell in my room typical of prisons and of those suffering from stomach and liver problems, I considered whether I should not wake him and accompany him down to the front door. It was a cold, wet evening. I was startled when Winkler came to his senses and, without saying a word, and at first going backwards, went out of the room; abruptly, it seemed to me. His case was difficult. I have not seen or heard anything more of the man since then.

afterwoRd: Crime stoRies

One of Thomas Bernhard's first writing jobs was reporting from the courts for a local Salzburg newspaper. That was in the early 1950s. Bernhard's interest in crime, crime and punishment, discipline and punishment is hardly reducible to his time as a journalist, given his earlier experience of institutionalization in boarding schools, hospitals and sanatoria as a child, adolescent and young man. Nevertheless, the conflicts of evidence, the nature of evidence not admissible in court, his own rewriting and condensation of cases as newspaper articles and items must have been a lesson in both the power and the limits and unreliability of the spoken or written word.

The seven stories published together here for the first time in English were collected in 1967 in a single volume simply entitled *Prosa*—Prose. All are concerned in one way or another with a crime, even if the crime involved is obscure or its revelation withheld from the reader for much of the length of the narrative. In *Two Tutors*, a shot fired from a boarding school window leads to the resignation of a tutor, even if the reader is unsure what it is that the tutor has struck with his gunshot. In *The Cap*, the story's impetus depends on the narrator's fear of an accusation of theft if he does not trace the owner of a cap he has found in the snow. In *Is it a Comedy? Is it a Tragedy?*, it is only more or less evident at the end of the story that the strange figure in women's clothes whom the narrator has encountered in a park near Vienna's Burgtheater murdered his parent twenty-two years ago. In the next three stories—

Jauregg, Attaché at the French Embassy and *The Crime of an Innsbruck Shopkeeper's Son*—the ostensible crime is suicide. Finally, in *The Carpenter*, it is an unspecified but undoubtedly violent act, the conclusion to a series of violent, brutal actions which has led to the carpenter, Winkler, being sentenced to a term of imprisonment from which he has been abruptly released before serving out his time.

These crimes may be the incidents on which the narrative turns, but Bernhard is more interested in the punishment which precedes the act legally defined as a crime: the sleeplessness of the tutor which has become unbearable, the incomprehension of the family of the Innsbruck shopkeeper's son who may or may not be disabled or disfigured in some way, but whose greater offence, in the eyes of his parents and his sisters, is that he writes poetry and is not fit to take over the family business.

The evidence, however, as elsewhere in Bernhard's books, is second-hand, if not third-hand. The narrators, whether speaking for themselves or another (the monologue in the monologue), are unreliable. Take *The Carpenter*, the last and longest of the seven stories in *Prose*. The narrator is a man of the law, a lawyer. First he relates how he is called on at his chambers by the sister of Winkler, the carpenter of the title, whom he was assigned to defend five years earlier. The sister announces that her brother wishes to speak to him and tells the lawyer of her brother's recent release, of her fear of him, of his difficulties with life outside prison. She flees the lawyer's office, her place is now taken by Winkler himself, whose account, diverging significantly from that of his sister, the lawyer now conveys together with his own responses. But the lawyer is himself a dubious witness. First he tells the reader that Winkler made the same powerful impression on him as five years earlier, then that the whole time his sister had been speaking he had been unable to remember what Winkler looked like, but remembered only his voice, then that he had entirely forgotten Winkler as soon as he had left the court building after sentencing—'I myself had forgotten Winkler the moment he had been led out of the courtroom . . . out on the street the Winkler case was no longer on my mind . . .' Indeed, the lawyer is alarmed because 'Winkler's attachment . . . dismayed me . . . it seemed to me both exaggerated and dangerous. It was as if in all the five years he had at all times remained in contact with me.' Yet, towards the end of the story, the lawyer mentions that only recently he had studied Winkler's prison file, concluding that there was no prospect of early release, even if he had formally petitioned the Ministry of Justice for just such a release.

These Bernhardian narrators, with their contradictory, long-winded yet breathless testimonies and self-defence, are reminiscent of

Kafka's unreliable, indecisive story-tellers, invariably pulling the carpet of certainty out from under the reader's feet. Bernhard's characters are constantly in motion—pacing, walking, running—yet this movement, this restlessness is revealed as, at best, circular. As the mysterious figure in women's clothes (which the narrator at first fails to notice) remarks in *Is it a Comedy? Is it a Tragedy?*: 'today he had, for eleven hours uninterruptedly . . . been walking "not up and down", he said, but "always straight ahead, yet as I now see", he said, "always in a circle. Crazy, isn't it?"' (The simultaneous movement and stasis in language that mirror the character's frustrated progress can occasionally, even in great stories like these, lead to a verbal log-jam which presents the reader—and the translator first of all!—with particular problems of dis-assembly.)

There has been a tendency, despite the distinctiveness of Bernhard's style, of his narrative form, to read him too literally in terms of biogra-

phy and of topography and place and less as a
reader (and writer) learning from other writers.
In an early talk on the poet Rimbaud, Bernhard
quotes a sentence, a sentiment which in its im-
moderate exaggeration could easily become part
of his own stance: 'I feel very bored. I have never
known anyone who felt as bored as I do.'

If the status and reliability of the narrators in
Bernhard's stories and novels has something in
common with those of Kafka, then it is also true
that Bernhard's rural (or urban) settings are only
superficially more specific than that of Kafka's *A
Country Doctor*. At any rate, the apparatus of
the modern world is hardly more present in the
stories in *Prose* from the 1960s than it was in
Kafka's stories written half a century earlier.
There's an express train in *The Crime of an Innsbruck Shopkeeper's Son*, a post bus in *The Carpenter* but otherwise no telephone, no radio, no
cinema. The litany of (real) place names absent in
Kafka but such a feature of Bernhard altogether,

their often comic repetition, as with Unterach, Parschallen and Burgau in *The Cap*, the apparent nailing down of place by names is something of a *falsche Fährte*—a false trail. If we were to tie Bernhard so closely and exclusively to his *unheimliche Heimat* (Sebald), then we would diminish the 'disturbance' of which his writing is capable.

Martin Chalmers